He wasn't going to let her get away that easily!

Trey stepped into the elevator with Madeline just as the doors shut. He detected a flash of surprise in her pretty face when he exited on the twentieth floor with her.

She halted. "I said, I can manage."

Trey shrugged. "I know. I'll just feel better if I trail along, make certain you're safe and sound."

"As you wish." Madeline turned on the heel of her black patent-leather pump.

"As you wish..." Trey muttered, as he took in the sway of her hips. The red dress was belted at the waist and fell over her bottom like a second skin. He wouldn't tell her they were neighbors. The aggravation of seeing her again might be more than he could stand.

With a final wave, Madeline unlocked a door and stepped inside an apartment. *His* apartment!

Talented and award-winning **Leandra Logan** is the author of five Temptation novels, all clever and amusing tales filled with unusual characters. This time around she decided to write about a woman who is extremely organized, a woman capable of undertaking huge projects and coordinating a myriad of workers under a tight deadline—in other words, a wife! To learn about running a "wife" service, Leandra took a community education course on how to run a maid service. She admits she felt a little weird being an undercover maid, but the experience only strengthened her admiration for these hardworking and ambitious women setting out to run their own businesses. So sneak away from all your piles of laundry and enjoy a very special treat, *Her Favorite Husband*.

Books by Leandra Logan

HER FAVORITE HUSBAND

LEANDRA LOGAN

Harlequin Books

TORONTO • NEW YORK • LONDON
AMSTERDAM • PARIS • SYDNEY • HAMBURG
STOCKHOLM • ATHENS • TOKYO • MILAN
MADRID • WARSAW • BUDAPEST • AUCKLAND

For the Fun Girls:

Ruth Williams McCarthy
and
Cindy Williams Mentes

The times were too cool
and the summers always endless.

ISBN 0-373-25591-8

HER FAVORITE HUSBAND

Copyright © 1994 by Mary Schultz.

Printed in U.S.A.

1

WITH CHARACTERISTIC impatience, James "Trey" Turner III was primed to leap out of the back seat of the taxi as it neared Skyline Towers, his apartment building. Traffic along Manhattan's Riverside Drive was heavy, as expected on a Friday evening, making driving laborious. Anxious to be back home after three weeks in Los Angeles, the advertising executive gripped the door handle, glad his last meeting had been canceled and he could get back a day early.

Not that he didn't enjoy the flurry of his high-stress, high-energy existence. He'd deliberately created his own circumstances when he'd founded his company, Creative Works. The up-and-coming advertising firm was now making its mark on both coasts. At the rate that his Los Angeles branch was blossoming, it would soon be on a par with his base here in New York. It was fortunate that Trey enjoyed the coast-to-coast commute. His frequent-flyer miles were racking up by the thousands.

The moment Trey's cab rolled up to the curb at the Towers, Martin, the night doorman, stepped through the stream of pedestrians to whisk open the door.

"Oh, it's you, Mr. Turner!" he said in greeting, peering in with a smile. "Welcome home, sir."

"Thank you very much, Martin." Trey leaned over the seat to pay the driver while Martin patiently waited on the sidelines, regal and attentive in his burgundy uniform. The Towers was an older building on the Upper West Side, and though made trendy by the many young professionals who lived there, it still held an air of understated dignity.

Trey swiftly braved the blustery November night, as did the driver, who rounded the car to open the trunk.

"So, Martin, how's the old homestead been holding up in my absence?" Trey asked, rubbing his gloved hands together.

A doorman for over twenty years, Martin smiled at the executive standing beside him in a gray topcoat and dark, custom-made suit. He always cracked a smile when Trey referred to the Skyline Towers in ranch terms. With a hand on his cap, he followed Trey's gaze up the old, thirty-story redbrick building. "The homestead, sir, is sound. Just as you left it." Martin turned to the taxi driver to accept Trey's garment bag and attaché case. "Shall I deliver these to your apartment? If you have a grill stopover in mind, that is?"

"Yes on both counts."

"Garment bag on inside-bedroom-door hook. Attaché on desk in study."

Trey beamed approvingly. "On top of things, as always."

The men exchanged a knowing look. It paid for Martin to remember the little particulars in this tenant's case. James Turner III rewarded those who did. He was a detail man inside out. Had to be, with dual businesses and residences. Not one for false modesty, Trey asserted that he'd become a financial whiz at thirty-one because of a shrewd system, a reputation for monied style.

He held the world by the tail with a few simple secrets for success. A loyal doorman and an efficient maid were all a young businessman needed for a stable personal foundation, for example. Doormen at the Towers had always been the best during his five years in residence. Unfortunately, a multitude of maids of all shapes and dispositions had come and gone over that same period of time. It was just recently—a scant sixty days ago—that he'd added the ultimate maid to his payroll: a woman named Ms. Clancy, whose sales pitch billed herself as "Just Like a Wife." "All the things Mom used to do—without the meddling" her advertisement had read. And it had turned out that she'd even written the clever slogan herself! As an adman, he'd been impressed beyond belief. She was a female entrepreneur extraordinaire, a lady worthy of his respect and trust—and three hundred of his dollars a week.

"Are you all right, Mr. Turner?"

Trey snapped out of his reverie to find the luggage-laden doorman watching him closely. "Oh, yeah. Just a little jet lag." With Martin on his heels, he headed under the entrance awning, feeling for some tip money in his pants pocket. Trey had a reputation as a generous tipper. When a reward was anticipated, services were good, he found. He treated his employees the same way. Bonuses for loyalty and innovation. Pink slips for lies and insubordination.

The two men paused in the middle of the lobby, Trey pressed some bills into the doorman's hand. "Nice to be home again, Martin."

"Yes, sir. You can take the man out of Manhattan, but you can't take Manhattan out of the man."

"Well said," Trey acquiesced. The men parted ways, Martin pausing to have a word with a security guard, Trey striding for the Skyline Grill entrance. As much as he enjoyed Los Angeles, and as content as his mother was after relocating there, he couldn't call anywhere but New York City home. He'd grown up here, and still thrived best in the hustle and bustle.

The Skyline Grill was a perfect example of the city's appealing after-dark atmosphere—loud and lively, spirited with an old, tattered feel. Not unlike a comfortable old shoe that molded to the foot just right. Trey eased through the glass door, and was instantly bombarded by smoke, music and the hum of conversation. The place *looked* a bit like an old shoe, as well, with its dark woodwork, hunter green walls, tarnished gold fixtures and creaky flooring. It was the sort of place that locals flocked to and tourists fled from. As always, Trey recognized a good number of the patrons, as well as the bartender and waitress.

"Hey, Eddie! Gina!" Trey saluted the gangly man behind the bar pouring margaritas into salt-rimmed glasses and the curvy blond waitress. Gina winked and whirled off into the crowd with her loaded tray.

"Well, well, if it isn't our favorite adman!" Eddie greeted him jovially. "Back for Thanksgiving, I suppose."

"Thanksgiving, an inspection by a potential client and, first and foremost, one of your special martinis."

Eddie winked in understanding. "Comin' right up. How about a roast-beef sandwich to go with it? It's only eight o'clock. Plenty of time to battle a bit of indigestion before bed."

"Sounds perfect. I'm so dead on my feet I could eat a jar of your horseradish sauce and still drift off like a baby." There were no free stools, so Trey leaned against the edge of the polished bar.

Eddie reached up to the glass rack overhead and pulled down a bowl-like piece of stemware. "I'm assuming you want a jumbo...."

"Is there another size?" Trey retorted with a laugh.

The bartender reached for a nearby pitcher and filled the glass to the brim. Trey took an appreciative sip. "You've still got the magic touch."

Eddie turned to pull a beer from the tap, then focused again on Trey. "So how's business?"

"Pretty damn good." Trey leaned forward to be heard over the din. "I'm on the verge of signing my biggest client. Harvey Swain, out of L.A."

Eddie whistled. "The father of frozen foods? I'm impressed."

"He's starting up a frozen baby-food line. Wants a fresh, youthful approach. Something to attract the nineties parent."

Trey grimaced when Eddie began to chuckle. He knew what was coming.

"Imagine that—one of New York's most eligible bachelors pitching pabulum on ice."

"Yeah, well, that isn't the crazy part." Trey grimaced with a swig of his drink. "Swain believes that behind every successful executive is a loving mate. He's a widower himself now, but he has a team of kids and grandkids scattered all over the country. Claims his family foundation made him the winner he is today."

Eddie shot him a knowing look. "I take it you didn't tell him we've got our heads together writing a swinging-singles book?"

"No, our *Permanent Bachelor Guide* hasn't been a topic of conversation yet." Trey held up his thumb and forefinger. "I am *this* close to signing him on, and he hasn't a clue that I'm not married. I just left the faint impression that I am."

Eddie appeared skeptical. "Would it really matter that much to him, Trey?"

Trey nodded solemnly. "He just can't see around that one blind spot. All the big shots in his company have spouses. I imagine some of them are marriages of convenience, but on the surface, the numbers are there. With the advertising game as competitive as it is, he could easily sweep a bachelor like me out of the way with one pull of the broom."

Eddie clucked unsympathetically. "Any operator who's dodged as many biological-clock-ticking women as you have should be able to sidestep one housebroken silver fox."

Trey winced into his drink. What a bleak description of himself! Was he nothing more than a single stud, stumbling through lukewarm relationships with no goal in sight? He and Eddie continually joked about dating and bachelorhood. It was a lark, a game. But whether or not life had anything better to offer was a question Trey sometimes asked himself in the middle of the night, or over a martini after an exhausting workweek. He'd nearly reached the engagement stage four times in the past decade, but things always fizzled out in the end. Some said he expected too much. But how much was too much when you were pondering a lifetime commitment? He took a gulp from his glass, swallowing his doubts along with the vermouth and gin. The last thing he needed tonight was to play the melancholy philosopher. He'd come in here to unwind, dammit!

"A continued cover-up is my current plan of action," Trey confessed conversationally. "I intend to draw Swain in with a splendid campaign, then confess to my single status sometime in the future. What better way to prove that an unmarried man can function to his full potential? Fact is, I really like the guy, Eddie. He's a very appealing client."

"You can swing it," Eddie declared, whirling to dig a bottle of wine out of the fridge for a sultry barfly at Trey's right.

Trey shrugged. "The suspense will be over soon enough. Swain is flying in here Monday for a cursory look at my main headquarters. If he likes what he sees, he's going to sign on the spot."

"Of course, you could make it easier on yourself but fast," Eddie murmured, his blue eyes twinkling.

Trey's brows arched in suspicion. "How so?"

"Get married for real." The bartender broke out in loud guffaws.

"Yeah, right." The raven brows lowered in a scowl. "After years of dating, I'm going to come up with a mate over the weekend. Besides, a sudden, foolish plunge into matrimony is the last thing on my mind tonight, now that I have my new Just Like a Wife on staff to handle my household," he proclaimed, the thought of her recharging him. "She makes the idea of marriage seem more unnecessary by the day."

"I still don't believe a hired wife can pick up the slack," Eddie argued, just as he had during Trey's last stopover several weeks ago. "Nobody's skirted the altar more often than yours truly, but I have the guts to admit there is something missing. My place and my calendar are a shambles. My cleaning lady shovels through once a week, but she sure doesn't make up for a devoted mate."

Trey aimed a thumb at his broad chest. "I tell ya, I have the best of both worlds. My Ms. Clancy is an organizational genius. She, too, comes but once a week, but is on call at all times. She has my personal calendar set days in advance. She sends flowers to my dates— find a real wife who would be so thoughtful. My kitchen is so sterile you could perform surgery in there. She even arranged a birthday party for my mother back in Los Angeles, by telephone."

"I'll bet she looks like Elmer Fudd."

"Who the hell cares!" Trey gave a carefree laugh. "The uglier the better—that sort are steadier in the long run. Won't end up at the altar herself then. Yeah, it's the perfect setup. Her magical maintenance leaves me free to howl and prowl my spare time away. If Miz Right shows up someday, fine and dandy. But I'm not in a panic about it."

"You're too damn cocky for your own good, Trey," Eddie complained. "You've never even seen this woman, have you?"

"Well, no."

"You've only been back here once since hiring her, haven't you?"

"Well, yeah."

"Then how do you know she's so great? Consistently great, I mean?"

"My neighbor Vic keeps me up-to-date on my 'wife's' progress," Trey swiftly replied with a satisfied gleam in his dark brown eyes. "And we do communicate—rather intimately, actually. There are conference calls concerning the TV repairman and the carpet cleaner. Better yet, she can fire off a fax that would make even you yearn for a vine-covered cottage, Mom's apple pie, a fluffy towel right out of the dryer...."

Eddie made a rude noise. "I just think that if a man wants those cozy amenities, he's got to strap on the ball and chain for real."

Trey grinned over the wide rim of his glass. "Not me. I'm free to pick up chicks anytime I want. In a pressed shirt and clean underwear."

"With that droopy mug of yours, I'd bet you're too damn tired to pick up a woman tonight," Eddie taunted, obviously intent on getting the best of him. "I say your jet set life-style's getting to you. That maybe Harvey Swain has a point about executives needing a family nest to recharge in."

"You just think you alone are king of the hounds," Trey shot back.

Eddie lifted his chin haughtily. "I am and will remain king of the Big Apple hounds. I have the edge over you, working like I do for the same hours in the same place every week. Women know where to find me. Face it, you've been losing ground for months," he asserted playfully. "I think I should get top billing on our bachelor's guide."

"The hell you say!" Trey pounded the bar top. "I'm in top form. Just been out of town, is all."

"Oh, yeah? Well, we'll just have to find you a conquest, won't we?"

Trey swallowed. "Right now?"

"Sure. A bona fide hound is always on alert."

"This challenge hardly seems fair," Trey grumbled into his glass. "Last minute. Without a shower."

Eddie scanned the jammed room, his eyes stopping at a booth along the opposite wall. "See that gal sitting all alone across the room? Red dress? Long blondish hair?"

Trey followed Eddie's gaze and inhaled sharply at the sidelong view. She was a looker. Sleek stockinged legs were crossed at the knee, displayed at a slant just under the edge of the table. Her button-up-the-front dress, fire engine red in color, was open just low enough to make a man speculate. Rounded cheekbone, slash of sable brow on creamy white skin . . . Trey's batteries sparked as he studied her profile, and he suddenly had to find out what color her eyes were.

"What the hell is she doing in a joint like this, without a man like me?"

Eddie stroked his jawline with a gleam in his eye. "Considerin' how long she's been nursing that glass of white wine and studying her watch, I'd wager that she's waiting for a workaholic guy a whole lot like you! Maybe if you wandered over there in that suit of yours, she'd mistake you for Mr. Right."

Trey rubbed the back of his neck, struggling with his case of jet lag. "If she were truly alone, I probably could swing it. But I don't think I've got the stamina to actually steal somebody else's babe tonight. A challenge like that would be more realistic tomorrow, after a good night's sleep in my own bed."

"I don't want to take unfair advantage of you, buddy. And I am just trying to help—to rekindle the spark in your dimming social life. Let's make it easy. You weasel your way into her booth to eat your sandwich, and I'll concede that you still have what it takes. Okay? No pillow talk, no phone-number exchange—nothing tough like that."

Trey groaned. "You make me sound pathetic."

"Just trying to ease you back into the saddle. And she is your type," Eddie said with a roguish look. "Bright, bubbly, beautiful."

Trey eyed his friend closely. "You know her personally, Eddie?"

"Just a friendly hello when she walks in," he admitted begrudgingly.

"Oh." He couldn't believe he was letting Eddie challenge him this way. Not when he was so weary and overwhelmed with business.

"She knows my name, so I figure she's a Towers tenant," Eddie went on to theorize, obviously adding more bait to the hook. "Been around for the last couple of months. Lunches alone on Fridays sometimes. Meets men in here. Guess that happens on Fridays, too—just like tonight."

Trey absorbed the rundown with doleful amusement. "Her name?"

Eddie shook his head as he paused to pour two glasses of vodka for a server.

Trey's annoyance mounted. "But she knows yours."

The bartender rolled his eyes. "Everybody knows my name. It's shouted out in here at least fifty times a night."

"You're the one who's slipping, Ed."

"Naw, I'm true to form, as always. Haven't hit on her myself because I like raven-haired beauties."

Trey paused in speculation. Eddie's excuse rang true. And it would be nice to meet someone new. With an impulsive surge, he eased back from the bar. "Okay, you're on. I'll give her a try."

Eddie grinned to himself as Trey moved through the crowd toward the lady in red.

"So, Eddie, you told him."

He turned as Gina rounded the end of the bar. "Told him what, my darling?"

The waitress tossed her mane of long blond hair back over her shoulder. "Told *him* about *her*."

"Trey claims to be the big hustler. He'll find out soon enough."

Gina's eyes grew wide. "But everybody in here knows—"

Eddie pinched her chin. "All the more fun for everybody."

Gina made a scoffing noise. "Oh, Eddie."

"Ah, he's such a wise guy. It'll be fun to watch him squirm."

"I thought he was your friend."

"Of course he is. What fun would it be to torture an innocent acquaintance?"

TREY RELEASED an involuntary breath as he hovered behind his conquest. Eddie calling her hair "blondish" had been the understatement of the century. It was a deep, rich apricot color, glowing golden under the muted light from the overhead lamps. She stiffened, as though sensing a presence. He swiftly stepped into her view with a cordial hello.

"Good evening," she returned shortly, studying the face of her watch a whole lot longer than she did his face.

"I wonder if I might have a moment," he pressed on, feeling suddenly rankled. She obviously wasn't the pliable type he'd hoped for, but he wasn't accustomed to being so easily dismissed by any woman. Especially one preoccupied with twirling the stem of a wineglass. Ouch!

He decided to wait her out and eventually got what he'd asked for. She tilted her face slowly up to his, meeting his eyes. Her face was heart shaped, smooth and pinkened and pretty. Her eyes were gray—silvery with tiny flecks of green. An involuntary tingle traveled up his spine as she proceeded to give him her full, undivided attention, leisurely inspecting him from head to toe. A visual physical of sorts. Without clothing. He'd done it to members of the opposite sex often enough to know the routine. He was flattered, disconcerted, and feeling just a little invaded.

"This isn't some kind of a pick up, is it?" she asked, a whole sixty seconds later.

He laughed in surprise. "No, no, of course not. I was standing at the bar, and Eddie suggested I stop over." When her sleek brows arched in query, he added, "You know—Eddie the bartender."

The eyes shifted toward Eddie and back again. They were a flatter gray now. Suspicious slate.

"You see, the poor sentimental guy considers all of his regulars family."

"And?"

"And he was hoping that you would be willing to share this booth with me for a little while—for meal purposes only. There isn't another empty seat in the house."

"Sounds like a pick up to me," she stated.

Trey rested a forearm on the back of the booth, closing his fist in a brief spasm of frustration. She was a cool one. Probably wearing dry-ice underwear! And acquaintances from the building were watching. Rather keenly it appeared....

If he walked off now, he could probably salvage his pride. But if he lingered and pushed, everyone would know he'd been attempting something more than a friendly hello. It would be around the whole place that Trey Turner was blown off by some hot babe tenant— on his first night back in town! Good sense told him to scram. But there was nothing about this lady that remotely touched his sensibilities. His eyes slitted, he leaned closer, inhaling her sweet perfume.

She turned slightly, her own nose wrinkling. It took all the patience he possessed to smile.

"Do you mind if I eat here? I won't tuck my napkin into my shirt or dribble down my chin."

"I am waiting for someone...." She trailed off in indecisive tones, as though he'd proposed matrimony and a new life in Australia.

That poor sucker of a someone. Trey pitied him, sight unseen. But he kept his smile steady—the stubborn, dangerous smile his employees had seen a hundred times. Trey Turner was out to have his way, and the world be damned! Why, the nerve of her assuming that this was a common pick up! There was nothing common about it at all!

"I suppose it would be all right," she said slowly, inviting him with an airy lilt of power, unaware of his rising temper.

Trey slid into the opposite side of the booth, nodding slightly at Eddie, who was watching from afar. No need to give him the satisfaction of knowing that this chick was instantly infuriating. A hands-off ice cube beneath her fancy wrapper.

He wasn't going to look at her—just because she anticipated perusal.

He wasn't going to let her *know* he was looking at her, anyway.

Dammit, she was simply too stunning to ignore.

Artistically applied makeup, for the city night-owl frolic. Flowing hair, deceptively styled to seem loose and free. A lot of women couldn't get away with that dramatic look, especially with the red-painted lips set in a smug curl. But she wasn't overplaying her hand at all. The boldness only enhanced her sexuality in an intriguing way.

Trey didn't like the slow burn that had started in the pit of his gut. But his hormones accepted what his intellect would not. This was a savvy city diva who roamed the New York City night like a supple cat on the prowl. Who called all the shots. As a man who preferred the soft, kittenish types, this was just the sort of woman he swung wide to avoid. And here he was, trapped in a cramped booth with her, intent on proving to his best friend that he was still a major-league player.

"As I was saying, this isn't a pick up," he reiterated smoothly.

"It certainly isn't."

One dark brow shot up. "Just what is that supposed to mean?"

She shrugged with her entire body, causing her red dress to ripple. "Well, genuine pick ups are done with more panache. Names are exchanged. Compliments are bandied to and fro. This arrangement is for the best, really. You, eating your sandwich in anonymity, peeking over at your bartender buddy. Anything less than a real attempt would be a phony, shallow gesture . . ."

"Trey."

"Excuse me?"

"My name is Trey. It's what my friends call me, anyway."

"Oh. Why?"

"Because I'm third in the family tree with the same name."

"Oh, really?" Her face brightened unexpectedly. "It just so happens that I like giving people numbers. Do it all the time."

She had to be mocking him. Toying with him. Savvy city diva. She was pulling him in and he couldn't bear to stop her. "You have a name? A number?"

She leaned forward slightly, as if to share a confidence. "My friends call me Mad."

Mad? He was sinking in quicksand, but he was too curious to climb to safety. "Is that an angry Mad or a nutty Mad?"

"Depends on the circumstances."

Indeed it would. Within the depths of those smoky eyes of hers, Trey detected a simmering witch's brew of both indignation and insanity! "So, are you waiting for a date, *Mad?*"

"A late date."

"Late as in tardy or deceased?"

Her mouth quirked. "I really wouldn't know that for sure yet, now would I?"

Her imperturbability was a thrown gauntlet to his ego. He resisted the temptation to reach across the table and muss her up. "You're a quick one, Mad."

"You're a strange one, Three."

"That's Trey."

"You're a three either way, are you not?"

"You do like numbers, don't you?"

"I don't think it's wise to reveal my likes or dislikes to you, a stranger."

"But I'm not a stranger. Most of the people in the place know me. I've lived in this building for several years."

Her creamy forehead furrowed. "I've never seen you before."

"Maybe because I have homes on both coasts." He paused, realizing that she was bullying him into a corner. "Come to think of it, Mad, I've never seen you before either."

"That's because I also have two homes. In a sense..."

"Bicoastal or astral?"

"By way of Tuckahoe."

"Ah, I see." He leaned forward, clearly on the offensive. "Perhaps I shouldn't trust you. How do I know you're not a dangerous, thrill-seeking suburbanite, waiting for the chance to slip something into my martini?"

"That's easy," she cooed. "You don't have a martini."

Trey chuckled. She was damn good. The more he tried to best her, the more his appetite grew for further challenge. Bad sign. He usually had a tight rein on a lady by now. "True, I don't have a martini yet. But it's on the way. How about a sandwich? How would you feel about one of those?"

Mad rested her chin in her hand, studying him closely in the dim light. "I think it would be far easier to slip something into the drink."

"No, no. I mean, would you like one of your own?"

She reared back with an indignant gasp, her savvy slipping a notch. "You mean now? Here? Out in the open, with you?"

"Well, yeah," Trey shot back defensively. "I've just spent half a day in airports and the other half on a plane. The only thing that kept me going was the thought of one of Eddie's roast beefs on white and two of his jumbo martinis." His voice grew ragged at the edges. "I'm asking you to join me for the works. Are we on?"

Mad's long, luxurious hair tumbled round her shoulders as she shook her head in wonder. "You just don't get it, do you? And you being a male!"

Trey raised his hands in bewilderment. "What am I doing wrong here?"

"You're trying to take my date's place, that's what!"

Trey twisted in the confines of the booth, casting a doleful look around the room. "Seems I've already done that, Mad."

"What if he were to walk in and find me eating with another man?"

"Maybe he would think you were hungry."

She released an exasperated huff. "Don't you have any feelings for your fellow males? A kindred connection with members of your own sex?"

"I like connections with the opposite sex better. You girls smell better and are softer to the touch." His gaze lingered on her gaping red knit dress. The bodice was unbuttoned about halfway, revealing a glimpse of lacy black lingerie. "What kind of fabric is that, anyway?"

"Lycra."

His eyes snapped up from her breasts. He'd deserved that description of her bra! But he wasn't about to admit the direct hit. "I see nothing wrong with you dining with me at this point. This guy must be at least an hour late by now. It would be a good lesson to him, to come in here and find that you accepted a second offer."

She clicked her tongue. "Don't know much about the girls you like to touch, do you? Despite those connections you have...." She trailed off, cleverly expressing both doubt and sympathy.

His mouth quirked as he willingly took the bait. "Just what do you mean?"

"I mean, no man would like to walk through that door to find me sitting here eating a sandwich."

"Oh, I don't know. You might look kind of cute doing it."

Her eyes lit up in challenge. "Ah, but if I'm caught doing it with you, he won't want to do it with me."

Trey leaned forward, his brown eyes simmering with intent. "Maybe I'll fill you up and you'll forget all about him."

She stared at him for a long, tantalizing moment, then broke into laughter. "What a come-on, Three! You really don't date much, do you?"

"Not lately." The confession came easily under her good-natured twinkle. "My business has been my mistress for the past few months."

Trey squared his shoulders as Gina appeared just then with his order. She retrieved Mad's empty wineglass, hovering over them expectantly. "And how are you two getting along?"

The question left him slightly uncomfortable. Eddie must have prodded her on. "Fine, Gina. But perhaps the lady would like something."

"Oh, all right," Mad huffed in surrender, gesturing to his martini. "I'll have one of those. Just so you won't look foolish."

"I'll tell Eddie," Gina promised with a smirk, easing back into the crowd.

Trey grimaced inwardly. Sure, tell Eddie that this chick was making a monkey out of him! "So, Mad, just how would I have looked foolish?"

"Why, by inhaling that sandwich in front of me, of course! And the pickles and chips," she added with a covetous glance at his plate. "And that fancy drink really would've called attention to you."

"It's exactly what you'll be getting."

"I should hope so!" she said, balking. "Boy, would you look cheap if I had a smaller martini."

Trey ran a hand through his dark, closely cropped hair. "Yeah, Mad, I guess I would. Hey, how about a pickle? A chip? Make me out to be a real Diamond Jim." He lifted his plate up off the tabletop for easy picking. To his amazement, she took him up on it. A bangled arm snaked out and greedy fingers grabbed two pickle slices and a hearty portion of chips.

Trey swallowed the last of his half of sandwich several minutes later. His second martini of the night shortly thereafter. "Mmm, great food. Eh, Mad?" He regarded her with a flinty look as she chewed, swallowed and dabbed her dainty mouth with a small cocktail napkin.

"You really shouldn't have let me eat half your dinner, Three."

"You really should've let me order you your own."

She hurried to drain her drink, the words ready to burst open like a dam. "I couldn't have my own plate! I shouldn't even have my own martini. Had my date shown up and found me with my own plate or my own martini—"

Trey held up one hand. "I know, I know. His virility, masculinity and overall self-esteem would've been irrevocably damaged." Finally saturated in curiosity and alcohol, he found the nerve to ask who was beating him hands down for this diva's attention. "Who is this special man, Mad—a movie star? Diplomat? Shipping magnate?"

Her sloping shoulders lifted a fraction of an inch beneath the fluid red dress. "I don't know for sure."

"You don't know his occupation?" Trey's brows arched in confusion. "Just how long have you been dating him?"

"Actually," she confessed with a glance at her watch, "as of now, we're two hours in the hole."

"You mean he's a *stranger?*" Trey's face grew thunderous. "All this fuss over an anonymous man?"

"Not totally anonymous," she retorted. "Such an idea! He happens to be a friend of a friend. My mother's acquaintance, actually. Lillian Fenderhoffer's cousin's nephew." At Trey's dark look she added, "Nice Tuckahoe family, those Fenderhoffers."

"You actually *are* from Tuckahoe?"

"Sure. You didn't think I flew in from the stars, did you?"

"No. I thought you lived here in the building and were putting me on about the rest."

"I'm a Tuckahoe girl who gets around, okay?" She grabbed her small black purse from the seat. "Would you like to see a picture of him? His name is Howard. Howard Fenderhoffer, and he lives right here in the city—"

Trey reached over and grabbed her wrist. "I don't want to see his picture. Just keep him tucked away in Tuckahoe!"

She snatched her wrist back with a huff. "Suit yourself!"

He shook his head and blinked rapidly. *Mad.* Whoever had named this chick at birth was psychic. "I can't believe you've made such a fuss over a blind date!"

Her lips pursed. "I can't believe you're fussing over my fuss."

"Must you best every word I say?"

She beamed. "Family trait. Big debaters, my clan. Always have an answer."

Debate nothing. It was called being deliberately difficult!

"Well, I really have to go upstairs now," she announced abruptly.

"So soon?" he asked in dry voice. "What if Mr. Fenderbender shows up?"

"Why, all the more reason to leave immediately!"

"But you've worked so hard to set the stage for him."

She regarded him with open pity. "It's too late, don't you see? I'd look like a desperate hunter at this hour.

Just as I would've looked like your charity case had I let you order me a sandwich."

Trey's rancor really showed as he envisioned her tossing half of his sandwich—teeth marks and all— back on his plate at the sight of her date. She would've done just that without a qualm. "Believe it or not, some women enjoy being in my company, eating my sandwiches."

"I'm sure they do. When they've been invited ahead of time."

"I couldn't call you," he growled. "I didn't know you!"

"Just the same, I wouldn't want my blind date to think I let you pick me up just because he was late."

"After two hours, I think we have every right to label that inconsiderate turkey deceased!"

Mad flinched a little. "I won't tell Lillian Fenderhoffer you said that. She thinks the world of Howard."

Trey couldn't help but wonder if Howard Fenderbender had gotten advance word on the "debate" in store for him. Perhaps Trey had judged him too harshly....

"Maybe if you dated more, got more experience in the game, you'd have more fun," Mad suggested brightly.

He grinned with gritted teeth. "I do all right as it is."

"Well, a woman has to play some games whether she likes to or not," she tossed back self-righteously. "And I'll bet you've pulled some nifty maneuvers to keep your business going. Same sort of razzle-dazzle, really."

"Not really. Business is a separate issue. Still, all in all, I am an up-front guy whenever possible."

"All guys think they're up-front." Her eyes glittered with devious pleasure as he swallowed the innuendo whole with a mighty gulp. "That's the one and only issue, isn't it?"

This was one dish that should be clearly labeled with a contents warning: Consume at Own Risk. Was it heartache or heartburn? His nerve endings were aflame, his pulse racing. All over the thought of touching this woman. Of kissing her sassy mouth to silence. Of running his hands up the smooth clingy fabric of her dress.

Did he want her or didn't he? Was it worth the aggravation, the risk of being shot down by a barrage of verbal bullets?

Maybe she had a bottom the size of Texas and he could forget her forever. He would soon find out—she was shimmying out of the booth. The place was as noisy as a Shriners' convention, but he still picked up the erotic rustle of her fanny gliding over the vinyl bench. It was the first bit of noise she'd made which showed true promise.

She was up. With the tight sort of buns California girls bared on the beach in those skimpy thong swimsuits.

It was hundred-proof libido that jerked Trey to his feet. He didn't want to know which apartment she lived in, he didn't want her phone number. He just wanted to walk her upstairs, a few paces back to enjoy the view.

"I'll escort you," he offered, fishing in his wallet for money to settle the check.

"No, thanks," she said lightly, scooping up her white, all-weather coat from the seat. "As I tried to explain earlier, I'm not in the habit of fraternizing with strangers."

"You! Not—"

"Thanks for the meal, though. Good night."

Trey balked for a second as she moved through the grill, edging her way to the lobby door. He hailed Gina and thrust the bill and some cash into her hands. "Got to dash."

The waitress nearly squealed in protest. "But, Trey—"

"See you tomorrow, honey. Say good-night to Eddie."

"But you don't . . ." Gina watched helplessly as Trey merged with the crowd, then hustled over to the bar. "You've got to do something!"

Eddie finished his transaction at the cash register and stepped closer to the frantic blonde. "What's the matter with you?"

"It's Trey. He sat with her all that time and still doesn't know. He's trailing her upstairs."

Eddie sighed. "What a bungler."

"Do something!"

"I'll call up to Vic," he decided, reaching for the phone. "He can referee the second round."

2

TREY EASED INTO the half-full elevator with Mad just as the doors were swishing shut. He watched her polished fingernail tap a button on the wall panel. Twenty. But that was *his* floor!

They made several stops as passengers entered and exited, Mad flashing him a smile once in a while. She stepped out the moment the doors opened on twenty. Trey detected a flash of surprise in her pretty face when he followed suit.

"As I said, I can manage." She halted her steps.

Trey raised his hands with a languid shrug. "I know, I know. I'll just feel better if I trail along, make certain you're safe and sound."

"As you wish."

She turned on the heel of her black patent-leather pump, throwing it into high gear down the left hallway.

"As you wish..." Trey muttered in nearly silent retort, his head swinging like a pendulum as he clocked the sway of her hips. The dress was belted at the waist and fell over her bottom like a second skin. They were on his side of the building, facing Riverside Drive. He wouldn't tell her they were neighbors. The aggravation of seeing her again might be more than he could stand, especially with the pressures his business was dealing him.

He slowed down a bit as he stifled a yawn. There was was no need for a face-to-face goodbye. Distance seemed the wisest way to sever this encounter. No clever closings, no bumbling attempts at a doorstep kiss—as if she'd let him try anything! It was over. Interesting, but fleeting. When he did set out to write his bachelor guide, he was going to warn men off this difficult type—the frustrating, argumentative sort of chick who shared her philosophies without invitation. The nosy, patronizing sort who dissected your soul, then scolded you for its contents.

Stranger, indeed! If he didn't deserve to walk her home, to enjoy the view of her firm rump, no one did.

She'd stopped near the end of the hallway. With a final wave, she inserted her key and stepped inside an apartment.

Curiosity got the better of him. He had to know her number—just to avoid her in future, of course! Trey counted off the doors, sure that hers would be the second-to-last one on the left.

He stood there dumbfounded for a moment, blinking incredulously. Raising a tentative finger, he traced it over the raised numbers.

How could he possibly hope to avoid this sassy diva when she'd just nested herself in his very own apartment?

"Psst!"

Trey had been tracing over the gold numerals on the wooden door for several moments when he heard someone behind him.

"What the hell are you doing, Turner?"

Trey slowly turned at the sound of the gravelly voice. A short, pudgy man in his midforties was leaning against the open doorway across the hall, his thick arms crossing his chest. Dressed in old jeans and a worn T-shirt, his frizzy salt-and-pepper hair in disarray, he looked as though he'd just stepped out of somebody's rumpled bed. Which was exactly what Trey told him.

The man looked down at his clothing, scratching his bristled jaw. "Rumpled is in when I'm playing the starving-artist gig—you know that. Just sold a portrait to an Italian countess not thirty minutes ago."

"Congratulations." Trey's tone was dry, but he'd never been happier to see anybody in his whole life. He was in the right place, after all. This was Vic Hess, his unconventional neighbor, a sixties' throwback making a living as a beatnik painter. It meant that Mad really *was* in his apartment. Unbelievable but true.

"Eddie just called from downstairs. Said you were bothered and bewildered." Vic stepped closer, his arms extended slightly in safety-net fashion. "Just how many martinis did you sponge up tonight?"

"Two." Trey peered intently at his friend, noting his shifty eyes. He had the answers, all right. "I think I'll just turn in now, if you don't mind. See you tomorrow."

"You can't!"

Trey nodded, his hand freezing near the doorknob. "This door's booby-trapped, isn't it, Vic?"

"Well . . ."

"You've been hiding things from me, haven't you Vic?"

"Well . . ."

"If you sublet my place to that nutty babe in red, I will take out an ad in the *Times*, telling everyone their phony beatnik has a masters degree in philosophy."

Vic gasped in panic. "I'll talk, Trey. Just come inside my place. Please." He wound a heavy arm around Trey's back and steered him across the hall.

Trey sank down on the lumpy brown couch. "So, who rented out my place—you or Eddie?"

Vic rubbed his palms together. "She isn't renting. She's sort of staying for free."

"What?" Trey shot up like a rod. Vic pushed him back down with a burly armed shove, and Trey rubbed his face with a groan. "I feel like I'm in the middle of one of my strange, horseradish-triggered dreams. Is that possible without falling asleep?"

Vic prowled the small living room like a stout, caged bear. "Where to begin . . ."

"Try anywhere," Trey directed in a snap, his eyes never leaving his prey.

"Okay. The lady in red. She's your maid, Trey."

Trey hooted in denial. "My Just Like a Wife? Get serious!"

"How did you hook up with her, anyway? I thought she was meeting a date downstairs."

"*You* thought she was meeting a date?" Trey echoed, realizing that Vic was totally serious. "You two share confidences, or what?"

"We're friends. I'm doing her portrait." He moved over to his easel near the window and turned it around. "See? Here is Madeline in oil. The beginnings, anyway. . . ."

Trey stared at the half-finished canvas with a murderous look. "That's where she belongs, all right. In oil! For a deep, bubbling fry!"

Vic set the easel back in place with a frown. "Oh, c'mon, Trey. Where's your sense of humor?"

"I don't see any humor in this—finding out this Mad person is my precious miracle maid, Ms. Madeline Clancy. My hired wife, with the organizational skills of a campaign manager, the tact of a U.N. diplomat and the habits of a Mr. Clean." He shook his head forcefully. "It just can't be true. She's efficiently run my New York home for nearly two months without a slipup. Charmed the socks off me with her wonderful faxes."

"I'm trying to give you the straight explanation. If you'd only let me finish—"

"There is only one possible happy ending to this tale," Trey retorted. "Tell me that Madeline has a naughty twin named just plain Mad. A tush-swinging vamp with the moves of a belly dancer, a confrontational chatterbox with the answers to every question ever asked in this universe."

Vic's raspy chuckle held an unmistakable note of sympathy. "Wish I could. But you gotta admit, the complicated personality you just described sounds, well—" he paused for a uncertain moment over Trey's thunderous anticipation "—exciting."

Trey closed his eyes, making a mental effort to superimpose the two personalities. His brows scrunched and his mouth thinned as he attempted the feat. Nothing. The two images simply bounced off each other—separate, yet equally vivid. Each distinct in its own way, drawing opposing emotions from him—emotions that he was certain could never merge to accept one well-rounded Mad Madeline.

"Didn't you even suspect, Trey?" Vic asked incredulously. "Didn't you exchange names, discuss your jobs?"

Trey shook his head in bemusement. "It's all a blur of red and lycra now. I do remember her passion for numbers...."

"Yeah, you're Five, you know. Maddy has a husband for each day of the week and you, being her Friday husband, are her fifth."

"Quit looking so damn smug about it all! That little master of aggravating debate could easily drive a wired man like me to the brink."

"I believe Madeline is more invigorating than aggravating," Vic confided loftily. "The sort of challenge any intelligent man would revel in."

"I'm too busy to revel."

"Too chicken to revel," Vic accused.

"Not chicken. Just cautious. Busy and cautious," Trey fumed. "That gal would never settle for anything superficial. And that's what I'm heavily into right now—safe, shallow relationships."

"But what about the rewards of complexity?" Vic queried seriously. "I know you dwell on those things. Sometimes, anyway...."

"Remember the last time I let my guard down?" Trey shot back. "I thought Bonny was a complex woman capable of serious involvement. Turned out she was looking for a sugar daddy, didn't it? Moved in with her *TV Guide* subscription, her remote control and a twenty-pound bag of gum drops. She wasn't deep or caring. She was a fake who got all her romantic lines straight out of soap operas and all her facts from game shows."

"She could've fooled anybody with that act of hers," Vic said consolingly.

"But she didn't fool just anybody," Trey lamented. "She fooled *me!* Made a monkey out of this grown-up businessman." He waved his hand with a sigh. "Let's face it, I'm no good at picking 'em. Picking 'em up, that's a different story. It's what I do best and what I'm destined to continue doing."

"Madeline is the sort who seeps right into a man's soul," Vic agreed with open pleasure. "Eventually, anyway. After seeping in everywhere else."

Trey shot him a lethal glare. "I can't believe you've been in cahoots with that she-devil on heels. Painting her. Schmoozing with her. Letting her use my place. And Eddie's no better," he railed. "Not only did he keep the secret, he steered me into her clutches—just to watch me flop around like a trout pulled up on the shore."

Vic shrugged his meaty shoulders, his eyes twinkling. "You told me to watch out for her, remember?"

"I didn't tell you to adopt her, dammit!" Trey exploded. "And if you're so intent on playing innkeeper, why isn't she nesting over *here?*"

"Because I am a sensitive artist who needs his space," Vic declared with a fluid wave of his big hairy arm. "A master of muse who erupts into work at all hours. I can't afford to have her primping over here every Friday night."

"Every Friday night? She's here *every Friday night?* Doesn't she have a home of her own?"

"She does have a home, out in Tuckahoe," Vic assured him. "She lives with her family there—"

"She's a *married woman!*"

"No, no. She lives with her mother, grandmother and siblings. Wherein lies the problem. Madeline needs a place to meet her city dates, away from the prying eyes of her clan. She's twenty-five and still feels that her life isn't her own. She has been using your apartment as a date stop. Perfectly harmless, really." Vic watched him thoughtfully. "So just how did you end up with her?"

"She got stood up."

"Oh, Lillian Fenderhoffer's cousin's nephew, Howard."

Vic knew even that! And it irritated Trey, deep within the caverns of his heart where logic could never reach. Madeline Clancy, alias Mad, was supposed to be his. At least on Fridays, she was. "If you two are that close, I still maintain she should be coming over here instead! Surely she can step around your precious muse, when it's out of its cage."

"Look, the muse thing is just part of it," Vic admitted. "There's the overnight part, too. I wouldn't want any rumors to start here in the building. Things are heating up between me and the spicy redhead down on the eighteenth floor. I don't want to lose her, not when I'm once again getting in the marrying mood."

"Mad's in the habit of staying overnight?"

"Well, sure. Always goes home first thing Saturday morning."

Trey sighed deeply, recalling the scent of his own sheets during his last stop home. It had been a Saturday afternoon—presumably a scant span of time between her departure and his arrival. He'd been dead tired and had flopped into bed for a short nap, to find himself engulfed in a most tantalizing scent. It had been her scent, left behind by that stunning body snuggling deeply into his covers. And he'd thought it was a new fabric softener! The Mad in the bar had emitted the same fragrance, he recalled. No wonder he'd been so entranced, so inclined to follow her upstairs against his better sense. His basic instincts had taken over at a whiff of the familiar scent, completely short-circuiting his brain.

"I'd like to believe the best of her," Trey said from the very bottom of his libido.

"And you can, Trey," Vic persisted.

He grunted with a small grin. "Quite a date 'n' dump operation. Very clever, leaving them down in the grill, as though she really has a residence here. She tried to do it to me, but I couldn't help but follow her."

Vic drew a sharp breath.

Trey raised his chin, regarding Vic in suspicion. "You're hiding something else."

"No, no," Vic denied impatiently.

"Does she have men overnight in my bed?"

"Of course not!"

"Then what part of the scenario do I have wrong? There's nothing left."

"You've got the basic scene, man. Madeline's very choosy—give her credit for that." Vic's tongue stopped in its tracks, like a locomotive that just overran the station house. He backed toward the kitchen, awkwardly offering Trey some espresso.

Trey jabbed his finger toward the floor. "Get the hell back here!"

Vic reluctantly retraced his steps. "You just can't leave anything alone, can you?"

"Not this," Trey admitted, terse with frustration.

"Okay," Vic said with a sigh. "Once in a while, if a guy has potential, she'll invite him in for a nightcap."

"So some of these guys do make it all the way up here, then."

"It isn't that high a climb, Trey."

It seemed like it to Trey. She'd tried to dump him like a hot potato downstairs.

"Does it really matter what Madeline's dating strategy is?"

"It shouldn't." But it did. She had gotten under his skin. The idea of physically desiring his platonic wife was confusing, disconcerting.

"Trey, you gotta promise not to hold it against her professionally."

His dark eyes hardened. "Don't you think I'm appealing enough to be invited up for a nightcap?"

"I think so," Vic soothed. "But the truth is, she's never dumped a guy in the grill before. They always make it to the door. No matter how big a dud she finds . . ." Vic halted again. "Don't take it so hard. You didn't even like her."

But he found her attractive. And his ego wanted a lateral response. It was a crazy part of her chemistry, the effect she had on him.

"You're okay with this, aren't you?" Vic probed incredulously.

"She tried to dump me in the grill!" Trey roared like a wounded lion. "Where does that put me on the dullometer?"

"I'd say below zero," Vic returned, a wry smile creasing his stubbled cheeks.

"I barely got a chance to prove myself!" he sought to explain. "Do you know how hard it is to make a point with her?"

"Does it really matter, Trey?" Vic interceded sensibly. "I mean, you really weren't her date."

Trey arched an ominous brow. "Oh, no? She ate half my dinner. Challenged every blasted thing I said. Add to that a nightcap, and you have yourself an authentic date."

"You're so hot for her that you're about to incinerate," Vic accused.

"That's ridiculous! I'm just angry and disappointed to find out that my hired wife isn't the cool, collected spinster type I hoped her to be."

Vic winced. After free-lancing for Creative Works several times, he'd come to recognize certain signs in the boss man. "I don't like the sound of this. You're going to use that nasty *I* word, aren't you?"

"Insubordination!"

"Yeah, yeah, that's the one." Vic rolled his eyes, shifting from one foot to another. "Can't you just settle this in a friendly way? Forgive and forget?"

Trey stared silently at the abstract mural on Vic's wall. It was a huge splash of confusion to him, just as Vic was. The artist just didn't understand about the boundaries a good businessman set up for his workers. Trey had a strict policy concerning employee loyalty. Madeline had broken that bond of trust by using his apartment as a date station. Invaded him, right down to the sheets.

"C'mon, Trey, have a heart. Madeline's worth her weight in gold."

That was undeniably true. She was always willing to go the extra mile for him at no extra charge. Sure, he knew there were other "husbands." But she'd made him feel like the one and only. "You know how I feel about business."

Vic circled the couch where Trey sat stiff backed and self-righteous, and wagged a finger at him. "You're just plain scared of her," he deduced triumphantly.

Trey openly balked at the artist's insight. "I have good reason to be afraid of her. Her impulsive streak is downright dangerous. What if it started to overflow into her job? Who knows, maybe she'd transform my apartment into a fruit stand, or a gallery to show your paintings."

Vic clapped his hands together. "Like, man, could we?"

"See, you can't even seriously defend her. And this particular week is crucial—for both of us. I am about to win the Swain baby-food account. You're hoping to do free-lance work on the ad campaign."

"Still—"

"Listen, Vic," he cut in with finality, "with Harvey Swain due in here Monday afternoon, I feel I already have my hands full. His line of nutritional baby prod-ucts is the kind of hot new item that could bring me real recognition. If he approves the New York offices the way he did the L.A. side, it's in the bag. I simply can-not afford to have Mad Madeline on my mind, to spend the upcoming week contemplating her fate. She over-stepped her bounds by using my place as her own, so she's out. It's a professional move, plain and simple."

"There's nothing professional about the decision. You're just ticked about not being invited up to your place for a nightcap."

Trey tilted his head back, closing his eyes. "Huh."

"Only a few make it inside. Honest."

"If anybody should be making it in there, it's me."

When Trey made a move to rise from the couch, Vic was right there with a detaining hand on his shoulder. "I think you should stay put for tonight. It won't do you or Madeline any good to have a blowup with your energies low and tensions high. I'm sure, in the light of day, with your head clear, you will do the righteous thing."

"I'm not dull," Trey grumbled, rolling his head back on the cushions. "You know I'm not...."

Before Vic could muster up a platitudinous response, Trey was fast asleep.

MADELINE, ON THE other hand, was very much awake across the hallway in Mr. Turner's apartment. This, of course, was his Friday, as all her Fridays were now. But this one was extra special, because he was due home tomorrow. Everything had to be in tip-top shape for his arrival.

Still wearing her slinky red dress, she took a tour of the small, yet comfortable living space. Seven weeks on the job and the place was showing all the signs of Just Like a Wife renewal. The kitchen floor beneath her stockinged feet gleamed in the faint glow of the stove light. It had taken weeks of patient scrubbing with a special fresh-lemon-and-ammonia mixture to lift the scummy surface from the classic checkerboard tiles, but the results were remarkable.

The windows were perfection, as well. She turned to meet her own blackened reflection in the pane of the sliding-glass door. Simple water and vinegar gave it and all the others a streakless shine. The new vertical blinds offered both privacy and measured light.

The bathroom revamping was another victory. The room lit up like sunshine when she flicked the wall switch. Amazingly, it had been a simple job of painting the walls, covering the pumpkin-colored paint with a semigloss. Vic Hess, her welcome, though unexpected friend from across the hall, had assisted her with the job, taping the woodwork and tile edges, covering the awkward nooks with brush strokes while she rolled the rest. Vic was a pal she and James Turner shared, the human link between them.

Until now. Madeline was going to make it her business to hook up with the successful, high-flying Mr. Turner this time around, no matter what. She simply had to have a face to pin on that charming, workaholic adman. It was bound to be a frantic week, with Thursday being Thanksgiving. All her husbands had special needs for the holidays, some more complicated than others. Heaven knows she could've done quite well without number Five zooming into town, into range of her pager.

Madeline stepped out of her shirtwaist dress right in the center of the living room. In black bra and panties she looked more like a seductress than a platonic spouse. But the truth showed in her shrewd gray gaze as she swept the room for those last details her husbands all loved so much. The crystal decanter on the small portable bar in the corner was full of the golden Clancy house wine. A fresh floral arrangement sat in the center of the table in an etched-glass vase, with a note about watering.

She inhaled with a rush of anticipation. Despite the inconvenience, she wanted him to come. Just as she wanted him to go away again soon thereafter. Missing a Friday here at his place—especially over the holiday weekend—wouldn't be too big a loss. But an extended stay on Five's part would spoil her long-range plan, destroy her social life!

After a quick shower, a nude Madeline crawled into Five's neatly made bed, taking care not to ripple the navy blue sheets. Everything was just right. The place was locked up tight. Her travel alarm was set for six. The bedside lamp was off.

Now it was time to rest. To dream. . . .

Ever so slowly she lulled herself into a heady state, replaying the unexpected encounter between her and that dreamy Towers tenant named Trey. The idea of him sleeping somewhere under the same roof as she—at that very moment—sent a delicious tingle down her spine. Causing the sheets to ripple, just a little. . . .

3

"YOU'RE IN BIG TROUBLE, Madness. Super-duper major goofball trouble."

"Says who?" Madeline dropped her duffel bag on the family room sofa the next morning, staring down at her little brothers, Peter and Benjamin, currently parked on the floor before the television set watching "The Flintstones." Twelve-year-old Peter had given her only the scantest glance with his announcement before turning back to the antics of Wilma and Fred. Five-year-old Benji had favored her with only a nod. A nod affirming the super-duper trouble.

Another weekend ahead with the Terrors of Tuckahoe. Living at home with her family at her age was becoming more and more intolerable. But for financial reasons and a host of others, there was no way she could separate herself just yet.

"Peter?" she called out above the chittering cartoon. "Huh?"

"Aren't you a little advanced for this sort of entertainment?" she taunted impatiently.

"Hey, even geniuses like me need some distraction. Besides, I have to keep an eye on Benji. Mom and Granny Dot went to the grocery store." He looked over his shoulder at her, his gray eyes bright behind his round, gold, wire-rimmed glasses. "And I meant it when I said you were wading in the deep stuff." With a sweet smile, he turned back to the television.

With an annoyed huff, Madeline marched forward to block their view of the screen. "Don't try to jerk me around. Not after the subway ride I just had. Without coffee! And I couldn't be in trouble. Not around here—"

"Don't start with that 'I'm an independent woman of twenty-five' stuff," he interrupted in a mimicking tone. "This is big. Way too big for that worn-out spiel. It's business, Madness."

Madeline placed her hands on her hips, hovering over the two blond heads in aggravation. She was going to have to pry it out of him. He wouldn't be a Tuckahoe Clancy if he didn't engage her in a verbal duel, didn't wring the last bit of drama out of the issue. It was their favorite form of entertainment—bantering until the last word was spent. Until they held not a bickering breath between them.

"Move your tush," Benji complained, tugging at the leg of her jeans.

"Not until I have some answers," Madeline insisted, remaining firmly planted in their line of vision.

"Give 'er the fax, Peter," Benji blurted out in anger.

"Fax? I got a fax?" She swiftly yanked the gangly boy to his feet. Hair fell into Peter's face as he grinned up at her.

"That's the fax, ma'am," he affirmed with a lopsided grin.

Sometimes it was so hard to believe that this skinny, twelve-year-old monster was taking accelerated courses in school. Despite his intelligence, he still had the emotional makeup of a preadolescent. "So where is it?" she demanded with motherly noises. "Down in my office?"

"In my pocket," Peter reported, stepping back as Madeline eyed him from head to toe. "You see, Benj dared me to fold it up as many times as I could. Didn't ya, Benj?"

"Yup."

"As you know, Madness, no Clancy has ever backed down from a dare."

"Nope," Benji squeaked from his position on the floor.

"Peter, give me the fax." Madeline shook his pajama-covered shoulders.

"Sure. As soon as you guess how many folds it took to reduce it to this size." With a wild leap, Peter hopped up on the easy chair, digging a square of white paper from his top pocket.

She advanced on him, eyes and mouth slitted. "Fourteen folds."

"Close, Madness, close." He leapt to the sofa as she lunged for him. Madeline landed in the easy chair with an *umph*.

"Is it the new paper or the old paper?" she asked, popping up to stalk him again.

"Now, there is an intelligent question," Peter congratulated her, stepping across the cushions. "It's the new stuff."

"Then I'd say it has seventeen folds."

"Right!" Peter tossed the square toward her. As Madeline palmed it in midair, the back door swung open, letting in a gust of cold autumn air.

"So the prodigal daughter has returned!"

Joanna Clancy, mother of the trio, breezed inside with a grocery bag in her arms. Like Madeline, she was dressed in a loose sweater and slacks. At forty-nine, Joanna was nearly twice her daughter's age. But with a fresh auburn tint in her long hair and some artistic strokes of makeup, she could have easily passed for Madeline's sister. As a young widow with a fondness for the mating game, she considered her assets worth preserving.

Granny Dot, on the other hand, was from the other side of the family. The mother of Madeline's late father, Robert Clancy, Dot looked every bit her seventy-three years and did nothing to conceal the fact. But she was still on the spry side. She stepped through the door after Joanna, carrying two grocery bags—and the car keys between her teeth. She promptly deposited everything on the counter, then leaned over the railing that divided the kitchen from the family room. "We could hear the hollering out by the garage," she scolded, homing in on Peter, who swiftly hopped off the sofa.

"Don't look at me, Granny Dot," he protested, attempting to aim the spotlight on his sister. "It's the champ who's down for the count."

"It was the blind date, I'll wager," Granny Dot said, running a hand through her gray hair. Her hairstyle had much in common with her tongue: clipped short and blunt. "Knew it would come to no good. I told Joanna it would come to no good when she set it up. Imagine, a Clancy stepping out with a Fenderhoffer." She clicked her tongue in disgust. "Left you at the bus stop on a dangerous corner, did he? Kept you out all night long, did he? Doesn't surprise me, whichever he did—him being from the unreliable side of the Fenderhoffers. The father's side, the ones who sold spoiled fish at the market back in 1963. Made the television news in 1963!"

"Well, he was unreliable all right," Madeline retorted, the folded fax momentarily forgotten as she stuffed her hands into her jeans pockets. "Never showed up." When confronted with twin glares honed to perfection by all the Clancys, which clearly stated *You should've called for a ride home*, she added, "I was fine. Met another man while I waited. Decided to spend the night at Five's apartment after all."

Granny Dot's lined face folded in a scowl. "A common pick up?"

A secret smile curved Madeline's mouth as she recalled his denial over that same accusation. "It wasn't a pick up. He said so himself."

"Was he cute?" Joanna asked in an excited gush, intrigued with romantic encounters of any kind.

"He was handsome," Madeline decided, picturing his face in her mind. "Direct brown eyes." Full of frustration. "Strong jaw." Rigid with intolerance. "Even white teeth." Clenched together to reveal a slight overbite. "A bicoastal businessman way too engrossed in his work, I must say," she revealed on a regretful sigh.

Granny Dot gasped in dismay. "I just saw something about those bi people on 'Geraldo'! They have big parties and dress up with earrings."

"Oh, Granny," Madeline said in amusement, stepping up out of the sunken family room and into the kitchen area with the women. "*Bicoastal*. It means he runs some sort of business with branches on both sides of the country."

"That ring any bells with you, knothead?" Peter cut in, seated again with Benji on the floor before the television.

"Don't start with me again about expanding my maid service," Madeline cautioned. "Every conversation you have drifts back to Just Like a Wife. It's not healthy for a kid your age to be so business oriented."

"We'll see," he predicted. "Right, Benj?"

"Yup." Benji's eyes never left the screen as he added his floppy nod.

"Tell us more about your date, Madeline," Joanna prodded.

"It was nothing much, really," Madeline murmured dreamily. "He was obstinate and opinionated—all the attributes a Clancy would admire in a man." She decided not to reveal his clumsiness on the dating track. His ineptness at the most basic strategies. It would only be fodder for this pack of polemicists.

"He sounds promising," Joanna murmured excitedly.

"He did have the nerve to trail me up to Five's place to see where I lived," she confided brightly.

"But you don't live there," Granny Dot interjected flatly.

Madeline ignored her. "I hope to bump into him again real soon for a second look."

Joanna beamed in approval. "Just how are you going to manage it?"

"Well, I'm dashing into the city Monday afternoon for a sitting with Vic. I'll just pop into the grill afterward. Trey claims to know the bartender in there—Eddie—rather well, so he should be able to give me Trey's apartment number." Madeline snapped her fingers.

"Then—whammo—I've got that man where I want him."

"Haven't you forgotten somebody?" Granny Dot drilled. A triumphant smile curved her thin lips as both her daughter-in-law and granddaughter regarded her. "Number Five, you flighty fools. James Turner. What happens if this Trey character comes a-callin' on you at Turner's apartment before you can get to him?"

Madeline's heart lurched. "Gee, I hadn't thought about that."

"Your mind isn't on your work is why," Granny Dot preached, turning to unload a grocery bag.

"Sure it is!" Madeline argued, her chin high. She worked damn hard to be the ideal version of the platonic wife: honest, forthright, chaste and dependable. Available anytime through her trusty pager. She spoiled her husbands rotten. Yes, they paid her well, but it still meant being confronted day after day with their messes and problems, their often-selfish demands. They all seemed like careless boys who would never grow up enough to make responsible husbands in the real sense. Didn't she deserve a little happiness for herself? A man who would nurture and cherish her in a purely personal arrangement?

"I can't devote my entire existence to these husbands of mine," she reasoned fervently. "I deserve a little private space of my own."

"The space you've been occupying is Five's," Granny Dot retorted.

Madeline knew she'd been infringing on Trey's unintentional hospitality. But his high-buck city apartment was her only lifeline to the city. To finding her own Mr. Right.

Madeline was anxious to find a real husband of her own. A man, full of passion and daring. Trey could be that man. He was certainly up to the verbal challenge, drawing out more in her than the average date with his ready wit and antagonizing demeanor. It was the sort of relationship her parents had shared. An equal-terms deal. Her father may have wished to be autocratic in his role, but the feisty Joanna had kept him on his toes until the day he'd been struck with a fatal heart attack. When an obstinate man could be trained, steered into accepting a fifty-fifty deal, it proved to be the perfect balance of unity and disruption.

"How did the evening end?" Joanna broke in to her thoughts. "Did you kiss him?"

Madeline frowned at the sea of fact-hungry faces. This was just the sort of invasive question that a Clancy routinely asked—and that an adult woman shouldn't have to answer! But answer it she would, just to close the issue. "There was no kiss," she admitted begrudgingly. "I eased into Five's door before he had a chance to try anything. I was already so embarrassed over Howard's no-show. Playing the woman of mystery was the only way to salvage my dignity."

Peter slapped his hand to his forehead and leapt to his bare feet again. "Wowee! This mess is sweeter than I ever imagined!"

Everyone focused on him.

"That fax I gave you is from Five," he reported with authority.

"What?" Madeline's heart began to pump frantically as she dug into her pocket for it. "Why didn't you say so right away?"

"Could it be that he's caught on to your overnight stays?" Joanna wondered with a furrowed forehead.

"Better hand that over to me," Granny Dot directed. "I have the best elocutionary skills here. Now, where have my reading spectacles disappeared to?" She squinted at Peter, who wilted a smidgen as she primed herself to ask the timeworn question: "Are you wearing my glasses, young man?"

The twelve-year-old made an agonized noise. "No, Granny. For the hundredth time, I am wearing my own wires. I couldn't possibly see through yours."

"They certainly *look* like my glasses."

Madeline favored her brother with a sympathetic look. As beastly as he could be at times, she felt he didn't deserve this latest round with Granny Dot. Granny had gone out and gotten herself a pair of glasses identical to Peter's. The poor preteen was mortified and hadn't invited a single friend over ever since.

Joanna intervened, putting a hand on her mother-in-law's arm. "Granny, I imagine your glasses are in your purse. I borrowed them to read that soup-can label, remember?"

"And yanked them back off when Craig Garnett came wheeling down the aisle in search of the creamed corn!" Granny snorted. "Such vanity isn't practical. Not on the cusp of fifty, Joanna. You should get a pair of your own."

Humor touched Joanna's pretty face. "I will. When I really need them."

"Fiddlesticks! Where did you drop my purse?" Joanna pointed to the counter near the sink, and Granny Dot shuffled across the linoleum.

"I had them first," Peter mouthed to his mother in a mournful whisper.

"Nothing wrong with my ears—just my eyes," Granny Dot called over her shoulder as she unzipped her bag. "*I* had them first. Back in 1947. After the war."

Granny Dot had probably had over two dozen pairs of glasses since then. She'd gotten identical glasses purely for controversial effect.

"This is my fax," Madeline announced with resolve as she unfolded the small square. "I will read it first."

"Second," Peter corrected automatically, despite his trauma.

"Third," Benji anxiously amended, desperate to be counted. "Even if I can't read, I know that Maddy's been fired."

"Fired?"

"How?"

"Where?"

"Why?"

Madeline ignored their cries of outrage, quickly scanning the message. "It just can't be.... I've been fired by Five."

"So he's finally found out about your shenanigans," Granny Dot chastised.

"Found out the hard way," Peter crowed, reviving nicely. "He was Mad's pick up last night. She locked him out of his *own place!*"

"Is this true, Madeline?" Joanna demanded in awe.

Madeline's heart stopped in her chest. The dashing Trey was the upwardly mobile James Turner III? "I'm always the last to know the important things around here, I guess," she murmured, dumbstruck as she replayed last night's events in her mind. Two strangers flirting. With no idea of how close they were linked....

"Madness spent a whole evening with one of her own husbands and didn't even know it," Peter explained. "Ate half his dinner and wiggled upstairs to sleep in his bed."

"How do you know I wiggled?" Madeline demanded sharply.

"Because you always wiggle when there's a good-looking guy around," Peter scoffed. As she opened her mouth, he continued, "And I know he was good-looking, because you let him share your booth. Says so right in the fax. 'I'm James Turner III, the man you shared your booth with last night.'"

Madeline blinked in disbelief. "My favorite husband, Number Five. Never a complaint, never a beep on my beeper, never a sock without a mate, never a bill collector to lie to. And now it's all gone...."

"Three hundred a week down the tubes," Joanna cried, snatching the fax from her hands. Together she and Granny Dot examined it with a series of moans and clucks.

"The odds of this chance meeting must be astronomical!" Madeline lamented.

"Your personal odds are somehow calculated differently in the cosmos," Peter pointed out in all seriousness. "Kooky and spooky."

Madeline pressed her hands to her flushed cheeks as she recalled her behavior, the wild way she'd acted during dinner. She never would've deliberately tormented one of her husbands. It wasn't professional. Only real wives had the right to go so far.

But on the lighter side, she couldn't help but wonder how James Turner—Trey—had taken last night's farewell. Oh, how flabbergasted he must've been when she shut his own door in his face! In spite of it all, she began to laugh over the vision, first lightly, then uproariously, doubling over at a picture of the arrogant fop in a martini haze of confusion.

The other Clancys watched her in surprise and consternation.

"I'm sorry," she said between gulps of air. "I was just picturing Turner, staring at his own front door in bewilderment."

"You're lucky he didn't kick it down," Joanna said. "Like in those historical novels of mine—"

"Oh, no, this man is too practical to kick down a door," Madeline assured her mother. "He'd have called a meeting to discuss options, called in experts, run it by the boys."

"You're lucky he didn't enter with his own key," Granny Dot expounded in horror.

"I bet he was just too rattled by then," Peter speculated with wizened practicality. "Don't forget, she'd been chasing him in conversational circles for quite a while down in the grill."

An issue no one tried to argue about.

"Well, you know what this means, don't you?" Granny Dot began, her large bosom expanding with her breath. "It means that Friday's Number Five must be replaced. Replaced by a bachelor right here in town."

Madeline grimaced, clenching her fists at her sides. She was primed to fight this battle. Monday through Thursday's husbands were homegrown Tuckahoe. Dot and Joanna had played a heavy hand in selecting them.

Number Five was different. Friday had actually been her day off until she'd decided to storm the city in search of someone. And when she'd found James Turner and his frequently empty apartment, it had seemed like divine providence had stepped in. Suddenly she had extra income, with a minimum of wifely effort and a date station to boot!

They all knew the purpose of Madeline's city connection was to seek out a real live husband of her own. What the Clancys didn't know, however, was that she was also shielding the hopefuls from them, intent on sifting through the potentials before exposing them to the family behind the woman. Such an extension of robust relatives could easily sabotage a new relationship in its fragile early stages. A man had to be toughened up before facing the family—protective Granny Dot, student to the steely Eliot Ness; flirtatious Joanna, who, in the company of a handsome man, could mistake their Tuckahoe home for Scarlett's beloved Tara; and the boys, who tried to wheel and deal their way into any visiting wallet with car washes and shoe shines.

She'd done a lot of fancy sidestepping before coming upon Trey and his apartment of opportunity. She just couldn't go back to meeting men at the drugstore down the street. Or the restaurant, or the movies. Or at the blasted curb!

Damn that James "Trey" Turner. For being pigheaded. For being attractive. For being flirtatious and seductive. Damn him for simply being one of her hands-off husbands! She couldn't fraternize with him now—it was against policy. As if she'd want to, knowing he was the sort of louse who would fire a girl by fax, without giving her a chance to explain. He was a coward. He was a lout.

He was the only husband she couldn't bear to part with.

She simply had to win him back!

With a sigh, Joanna glanced back down at the fax. "It says here you are to come to his office promptly at nine Monday morning, and bring his house key. So how are you going to handle this, with One expecting you at his house for a thorough cleanup. Don't forget, his folks are due back for the holiday weekend."

"Can't afford to lose One because you're busy being fired by Five," Peter put in.

Madeline sighed. "I'll call One right now, arrange something for Sunday. Guess not even my day of rest is mine anymore."

"I suppose we should hightail it back to the grocery store today," Granny Dot said. "Tack an index card on the bulletin board advertising for a new Number Five."

"Not so fast," Madeline exclaimed. "I'm not ready to weather my first divorce just yet. This happens to be one marriage of convenience worth saving!"

4

TREY TURNER WAS UP at 5:30 Monday morning for a few laps around the Central Park reservoir. He mentally sorted out his schedule as he pounded along in an easy jog. It was imperative to make the most of the short holiday week ahead. He had a quiet Thanksgiving planned for himself, like last year and the year before that—he intended to work through the weekend in the solace of his apartment. The fact that he had nowhere to go for turkey really didn't enter into his decision, either. Once he landed in the office this morning, he would be playing catch-up. He'd sew together the loose ends, getting ready to head back to Los Angeles in a few weeks' time. It was the merry-go-round he lived on.

Harvey Swain's impending visit was the first order of business. And his New York crew, from the director of marketing services to the head of the production department, knew it.

Everybody right down to the clerk typist was on alert to be at their very best. The right clothes—presentation clothes, he called them—were in order for his key personnel. True, Trey had nearly ironed out the Swain Frozen Foods baby-food campaign in Los Angeles, but he wanted everyone primed for the pitch. Even if it might be just wishful thinking. . . .

Trey was impressed with Harvey Swain and the way he'd taken his father's fledgling frozen-food business which had been a rinky-dinky operation in the sixties, making it a household name by the midseventies. At the age of fifty-eight, when many men were slowing down, Swain was gearing up, determined to expand into the baby-food market, offering a variety of convenient, single-serving fruit and vegetable packets for the mother on the go with a sharp eye on her child's nutrition. He was a brilliant man with big ideas.

The moment Trey heard Swain was shopping for a bright young advertising firm to handle the new account, he'd jumped through hoops to get his attention. Creative Works ended up in the running with two other top-notch West Coast agencies. Swain had claimed that he was looking for something fresh and innovative to make a mark in the incredibly competitive infant-food arena. And the agencies—Creative Works included— had believed him, building their presentations around nineties values. What Trey soon found out was that Swain only *thought* he wanted something fresh. Trey's ideas centered around today's parents, the return to family values. Apple trees and sunshine and healthy children frolicking. Swain's vision was a tunnel one, centered on one final end.

Harvey Swain wanted his own picture on each and every package of baby food. As ambitious and energetic as he was, he was secretly dwelling on his own finite fate. He'd become bullish on the idea of joining the ranks of Betty Crocker, Ben and Jerry, and Paul Newman, of becoming a figurehead on one of his own products, a character who would forevermore smile back at everyone who ever opened a freezer door for the benefit of their tot. And then there were the commercials. He wanted to saunter into a kitchen himself to speak, an old-fashioned kitchen with a new-fashioned freezer full of Swain's Frozen Foods.

The other agencies had fought him tooth and nail, feeling that Swain's heyday was over. But Trey genuinely didn't think so. He had hopes for the project because he felt that Swain's product was inspired—so much so that there had to be some route of compromise. Luckily, Swain sensed his sincerity, and was on the verge of signing on with Creative Works. Swain had claimed that one look at the New York office would satisfy him completely. Trey hoped to use the inspection time to make some fresh pitches, sway him over to a new avenue of thinking. The staff in his New York office was the most aggressive one, a brainstorming troop that worked well under pressure. Trey smelled success.

Except for that nasty little glitch that made his blood boil—Harvey Swain's preference for married executives—with offspring, whenever possible! The old coot felt a stable home life rounded off the busy professional, and he wasn't about to make an exception, not with his own family foundation to back up his theories.

Why, the notion was as outdated as the horse and buggy! As archaic as Swain's dopey ad campaign! Not everyone snared the perfect someone. And settling for less—as many people seemed to do—was no option at all for Trey. Old-fangled ideas meant old-fashioned prejudice, in his mind. It was totally unfair.

Trey felt he had the right to tell a little lie under the circumstances. It was the principle of the thing. And he thought he'd solved his own dilemma quite nicely.

Taking on his maid, Madeline, as his mythical wife had seemed like the obvious, logical step.

It had just fallen into place, with all the faxes zipping back and forth between them. She'd been the perfect mate, on paper—smart, efficient and cheery. Swain was impressed with her way of running things back home in New York. It had been Trey's intention to waltz Swain in and out of the Big Apple without ever seeing Madeline. And that part of the plan was still firmly in place. After today *he* would never have to see her again, either. But forgetting her . . .

With heart-pumping irritation, Trey picked up his pace on the reservoir path. He trotted up behind a woman in a form-fitting orange tracksuit—inappropriate dress for the chilly morning air. She was wearing it for effect, of course, just as Mad had done with her outfit the other night. Trey swiftly overtook the woman, hoping to dismiss the images she evoked.

Imagine, his Just Like a Wife behaving like a siren, using his apartment as a mantrap. He had to forget her. He would forget her.

Yet she was the most intriguing blend of contradictions he'd ever encountered, with her domestic skills, warm fuzzy support and—shockingly—her white-hot sensuality and determination to be deliberately difficult. God help the other four unwitting husbands who kept on this insubordinate employee. God help the man who ended up with her off-hours!

WHAT DOES A WIFE WEAR to her first divorce?

Especially when she wants her man back in the worst way?

Madeline looked coolly chic as she rode the elevator up to the floor housing the Creative Works Fifth Avenue offices. Her suit was aqua linen, her blouse a dark cream silk. The shoes were low, sensible black pumps and her lush golden orange hair was caught back in a neat French braid. The outside wrapping did indeed reflect the sought-after sophistication. There was no outward clue that Granny Dot had tacked her hemline at knee level with masking tape or that the nimble fingers that had styled her hair belonged to Benji, the knot-tying hobbyist of the clan, or that her ever-nubile mother, Joanna, had touched up her face with sub-dued makeup, all the while coaching her on maintaining a soothing, modulated voice.

Unfortunately, as hard as they all tried, none of the controversial Clancys could coach her on the protocol of delivering an apology. Even when—as Madeline assured them—the apology was as phony as a three-dollar bill, as superficial as a business maneuver could be.

All heads had turned to Peter, the king of the Clancy operators, but even he couldn't come through. The Clancys were always right in the first place, were they not? he challenged. Why, apologies went against the grain of everything they stood for. No matter what they happened to stand for at any given moment. With that impassioned soliloquy off his chest, he'd trotted out to join the kickball game in the street on this first day of Thanksgiving vacation.

Yes, the Clancys would be an acquired taste for the real live husband in Madeline's future. All the more reason to make this bogus husband see reason. She was reconciled to the fact that she could not have the hunky Trey Turner in her life. But she simply had to have her Friday job back—and his apartment! Her husband hunt had to continue in the city.

If she could just round off today's wifely image with a little sincerity.... "I'm sorry," Madeline mumbled under her breath. "So sorry. So very, very sorry." She worked on the timbre of her voice, running the spectrum of emotion, searching for just the right sound, as though she were tuning a piano. Every attempt sounded pandering and tinny. But, damn it all, she'd never crawled before in all her twenty-five years. Self-contempt, for the briefest moment, outweighed her contempt for Trey Turner. She was nothing but an apple-polishing, ring-kissing jerk!

But her survival instincts soon quelled such useless recriminations. Joanna and Granny Dot were already searching Tuckahoe for a new Number Five. A backup if her crawling didn't work.

"I am so, so sorry," she announced in a clear voice dripping with desperation.

Even the jaded city dwellers sharing the elevator couldn't ignore this fervent proclamation. A tall, distinguished man in a gray topcoat and hat turned to regard her with sympathy. "Are you all right, miss?"

Madeline smiled up at him, brushing aside her wispy bangs. "Oh, yes. Certainly. But can you tell me, sir, did I sound contrite?"

Looking a trifle nonplussed, he turned to the small, plump female on his left for her opinion. She leaned over with a kind look. "You sounded just fine, dear. You work here in the building?"

"No, just visiting."

"Man trouble," the man said with a shadow of a smile.

Mad's nod was swift and sure. "Exactly."

"Well, I just hope he's worth it," a young lady chirped from behind.

Madeline tried a few more apologies on them before reaching Turner's floor.

"Good luck with the boyfriend," the man in gray said as Madeline stepped through the doors.

"Actually, he's more a husband than a boyfriend. My fifth, actually," she attempted to explain to the open-mouthed passengers as the doors slid shut on them.

Creative Works proved to be a busy suite of offices. As she crossed the carpet to the reception desk, Madeline felt like a tiny cog in an animated scene of moving bodies, humming voices and glowing computer screens. Until she announced herself to the young, red-headed receptionist. Suddenly the place went nearly dead, except for the phones, which bleated on without relief. Heads bobbed up from behind partitions, faces popped out of doorways. People on foot froze in their tracks. There was no surprise in their honed, professional expressions. Just anticipation....

Madeline swallowed, shifting her black leather sack from one shoulder to the other. Did everyone here know how she'd been unceremoniously sacked? How many of them had read the perky faxes she'd sent to the Los Angeles office? And why the heck should she care? It wasn't like her to care. This was *business!* She had no feelings for this lug of an adman. Sure, he'd shown some potential back at the grill, but she needed a man who felt the big sledgehammer fall at the sight of her. It would take that sort of chemistry to endure the whole Clancy package.

Madeline's eyes fell to the desk before her. The name plaque read Sue Parker. "Sue, exactly when will Mr. Turner have time to see me?" she inquired with aplomb.

Sue grabbed the phone and punched in a two-digit number. "She's here, boss."

She? The woman made it sound like an urgent password.

She set the receiver back in place like a hot potato. "He's coming!"

Madeline felt a surge of hope. Maybe all of them were on edge because he desperately wanted to right his wrong. Maybe he'd spent the weekend wondering what he'd ever do without her!

The first door along the hallway swung open and Trey burst into the reception area in a dark suit and white shirt. Madeline involuntarily inhaled in appreciation. Trey Turner held power in his carriage and authority in his tanned, chiseled features. His hair had been clipped since Friday night, in one of those imperceptible high-buck haircuts that weren't supposed to look like haircuts.

If only she didn't know about his trifling ways, his endearingly awkward come-ons. One look at his handsome face brought all the original sparks back. Madeline's knees went weak from the impact. He was an absolute dreamboat, just as she remembered. But first and foremost, he was an irate ex-husband. She'd do well to remember that. To remember it was her job she was after.

Trey swiftly perused his people with a look of consternation. "This isn't a sideshow."

Madeline shared his irate feelings, but for a different reason. The females here were employed by Trey—were still employed by him. They hadn't mistakenly fallen under his spell. Hadn't been wooed, then booed. Amusement danced in their eyes. But Madeline was sure Trey had never put them in such an awkward dilemma. From her weeks as his "wife" she knew him to be full of integrity and too immersed in his business to deliberately view his employees as anything but drones who helped him put out the work.

He approached the receptionist with quick strides. "Sue, draw up that item we discussed. And as for the rest of you, be on your toes. And remember, Operation Matrimony is in motion as of now." With a parting glower, he waved Madeline back to his office.

Madeline flinched as he ushered her inside, slamming the door behind them. Operation Matrimony? It might be too late to patch all this up, after all. If he had a real wife in the wings, he wouldn't want his hired one back. And if he was on the brink of marriage, what had he been doing flirting with her in the Skyline Grill?

Trey moved into the room, his hands in his pockets. "Sorry they all know," he said, raising his eyes to the ceiling. "This sort of thing is manna for office gossips. Employee insubordination."

She smiled in forgiveness. He was already on a defensive—at least a smidgen. "I'm sorry, too, Mr. Turner," she said in the sweet voice that had gone over so well in the elevator.

"Sorry you got caught, you mean!"

Madeline glared at him huffily as he erupted like a volcano before her eyes. He sure hadn't climbed the corporate ladder with too many outbursts like this under his belt. She had to be getting under his skin.

"Look, Five, I came here to apologize!"

"You came here because I told you to!"

Madeline's face soured. This buttering up stuff was tougher than she'd ever dreamed possible, but her precious freedom was at stake. She'd never get to the city on a regular basis if she had yet a fifth husband in Tuckahoe! Of course, the first order of business was to find out what Trey had been talking about in the outer office. No sense in even bothering with all this if he was planning to marry.

"So, what is this Operation Matrimony stuff?" she asked boldly, tossing her leather sack on a winged chair. "You aren't getting married yourself, are you?"

Trey reared back, a ferocious glint in his brown eyes. Could she be now attacking his mating skills as she had his dating skills? The same savvy diva smugness was there in the curve of her mouth. "I suppose that would surprise you, being that you've judged me one incompetent lady-killer."

She lifted her shoulders. "One never knows who has the killer instinct, I guess."

"You might do well to remember that," he advised. "Your habit of pushing a conversation to the brink of insanity might just be your downfall one day."

"So, are you or aren't you? Getting married, I mean."

"I am not. *Not ever*. Don't believe it's a necessary step."

"Whew! That's a relief."

Trey frowned in bemusement. Did she ever respond to anything predictably? Surely she'd expected him to defend his right to a happy married life. Unless...unless she expected her job back and wanted him single! Ah, so that was it. She was here to grovel. How interesting.... He would enjoy this. A lot.

Madeline's lush brows arched in a moment of uncertainty as she attempted to read his wizened expression. "Please understand, Mr. Turner, I'm here with an olive branch in hand. I'm hoping we can iron out our differences and you will see your way clear to rehiring me."

"Look, *Mad*." He enjoyed saying it. Labeling her for what she was. Their verbal tussle in the grill had tormented him all weekend long. He'd replayed her snappy comebacks over and over again. Rehearsed the things he should've said. He wanted nothing more than to relive that night. He wanted nothing more than to forget that night. Hell, he didn't seem to know his own mind at all!

"Look here, " he reiterated with a jabbing finger. "I sent you a fax ahead of time so you would be reconciled to your fate by now."

"Seems like dirty pool to fire somebody by fax," she muttered in complaint.

"Why? It's the way we've done most of our communicating to date."

"It's so cold. So absolute."

"No chance to talk me out of it, you mean," he cut in smartly. "I assure you, the results would be the same no matter what method I used. No matter what arguments you were to pose."

Madeline stomped her foot on the carpeting. "I deserve the chance to defend myself!"

Trey glanced at this watch with Swain in mind. About two hours until his arrival. "Will it get rid of you?" he blurted rudely. "If I let you speak, let you tie me up in knots again with your tongue, will you give my key back and go?"

"If you decide you really want your key back—"

"Mad..."

"Yes, scout's honor," she hastily assured him.

Trey rested a lean hip against the edge of his desk and folded his arms across his chest, bracing himself for the show. She began to move around the room slowly, like a lawyer hoping to hypnotize a jury. But there was nothing judicial about her appearance. Amazingly, even in this office setting, under the fluorescent lights, Madeline still had an alarmingly tangible sensuality about her, from the easy sway of her hips to the pucker of her full mouth. Sure, she'd tried to camouflage it by covering her curves in a boxy suit and taming her wild apricot hair in a sleek twist. Unfortunately, the attempts at restraint made her all the more sexy.

His eyes dropped to the safe territory of her sensible shoes, then involuntarily rose up the length of her stockinged calves to her hemline, where her knees skimmed linen, offering a tantalizing peek of thigh. Trey rubbed his furrowed forehead in irritation. He was actually being turned on by a pair of knees! Insubordinate knees. He'd never even thought much about knees before. He loved a supple leg, but to pinpoint a *knee*...

It was preposterous! Especially with Swain nearly on his doorstep and Madeline about to be bounced forever from the same.

"I'm going to level with you, Five."

"Mr. Turner to you."

"Until you have your key back, you're still officially Five!" she insisted, pounding the chair back. "Anyway, this is how it is. I simply have to be your wife." She paused, hating this next part—having to reveal some of her soul to this Fifth Avenue power monger. "I happen to believe very strongly in marriage, Five. I want a husband more than anything in the world." She averted her eyes, attempting to break contact with his penetrating gaze. "As it's turned out, you're my ideal—"

"What?" he squawked in panic.

"Ideal client," she clarified. "Surely you don't think I fell for you the other night!"

Trey hid his bruised ego behind slitted lids. "I see."

"Well, see that you do. I'd never consort with one of my husbands. It's your *place* I want. In the midst of the action." Her eyes began to shine as she embellished on her scheme. "It gives me the pick of the city litter, you see. The chance to cast a line in the biggest man pool around. Sure, there are nice guys in Tuckahoe, but I just think it wise to increase my odds of finding my perfect mate to the max."

"Do you realize you've given me reasons that benefit only you?" he scoffed in amazement. "What about me, the employer?"

"Naturally, my assets are already known to you," she persisted matter-of-factly. "I'm good at my job. It's just a matter of helping each other out. Being the best we can be."

Just as Trey opened his mouth to respond, a muffled beeper sounded.

"Oh, not now!" Mad rounded the chair, and with jerky motions unzipped her purse and extracted a pager. With a quick look at the phone number displayed on its tiny screen, she said, "Number Four is trying to reach me. May I use your telephone?"

"By all means," he invited with an extravagant wave toward the one behind him on the gleaming mahogany desk.

"Four's the odd man out this week, with his regular Thursday being Thanksgiving," she explained, plopping her purse beside the phone on the desk top. "I promised we'd iron things out today."

Trey watched in awe as Madeline pulled her large clip earring off her ear, slid the receiver into the crook of her shoulder and punched in a number.

The transformation as she spoke to number Four was incredible. This was the Madeline he'd envisioned from afar—collected, reliable. If she hadn't had that hint of shimmy in her walk, he might have believed her alluring body language was a miscommunication. But, oh no, Mad did everything with deliberate forethought. She was trying to sell the whole package, with an obvious leaning to her wifely capabilities. But she couldn't resist the sexual overtone. Dangerous chick. High-voltage trouble. His next maid would be interviewed in person. Rigorously.

"Yes, Four," she said placatingly, with the professional lilt he recognized from their own phone calls. It was nothing like the seductive purr she'd used on him in the grill. She dug a thick loose-leaf binder out of her bag and started thumbing through it. "I can work you in Wednesday afternoon. No, no, it's no trouble at all. I spoke to Three yesterday and he says his needs are light this week.... I know you do," she purred with an intimate laugh, flipping a page in the book. "But with your sister visiting, I understand the urgency. Yes, the flowers are taken care of. As are the groceries. And the carpet cleaners would like to come tomorrow. Noonish.... Okay, I'll confirm. Bye." Madeline hung up the phone, busily tucked away her book and replaced her earring. "So where were we, Five?"

"I believe you were discussing your assets."

"Yes, of course," she concurred with a slight jutting of her chin. "So, shall we give this another go?"

Trey's jaw slacked a mile. "You don't seem to understand, Mad. I don't like the way you used my place as a pick up stand! And what you're telling me here is that you want to go right on doing so!"

Her rich brown brows narrowed fiendishly. "I don't do pick ups, mister. Nobody should know that better than you—a man who failed so miserably at the job the other night!"

Some job-salvaging mission! Trey squinted as anger burned his vision, outlining Madeline and everything around her in electric yellow.

"I did not try to pick you up!" he growled through gritted teeth. "And we both know you ditched me only because you decided I wasn't quite right for you. What happens, Mad, when a man *is* right?"

"Gee, I don't know...."

"Well one of these days, someone will rise above 'dudster' status," he pressed on, his control slipping. "Then what will my apartment become? Will the date stand stay open long after the nightcaps are gone?"

Humor touched Madeline's features. "Vic told you about the dud stuff, didn't he? I mean, you wouldn't have chosen the word *dudster* on your own. It's not one you hear every day. Now *jerk, creep*—those words you hear a lot in women's health clubs. But they're too harsh for any date of mine. To get as far as meeting me in the grill a man has to be above those tags."

"I am not a dud!"

"I never said you were!"

"You didn't invite me in for a nightcap!"

"Why didn't you invite yourself in? You had a key, didn't you?"

At mention of the key, Trey's dark eyes glittered. "I believe that's where this ends, Mad. With my key." He extended his huge palm, holding it right below her heaving breasts.

She wanted to give him a sock in the chops as he hovered over her with that superior look on his gorgeous face. Anger surged through her system as she thought about how easy it must be for him to get a date anytime he wanted one. He didn't need polished lines to garner attention. Didn't need a gimmick, like she did.

"Well?" Trey demanded as she turned to rummage through her purse.

Her key to the city. She plucked it out and pressed it into his palm, without the fanfare with which Vic had presented it to her eight short weeks ago on Trey's behalf.

"Thank you very much, Madeline. You can pick up your check at the reception desk out front."

"Feel free to pick up a heart the next time you're at the hospital," she sassed back, the last of her beguiling act falling to the floor like a discarded cloak.

Her emotional attack seemed to shock him. "This is *business!* Didn't your mother teach you anything about surrendering with grace?"

Madeline made a noise of disgust. "Why, the Clancys of Tuckahoe never quit. We're tossed around, beaten down. But we *ne-vah* quit!" With that parting shot, Madeline whirled around and strode from the room, her butt swinging to a nonexistent bongo-drum beat.

5

WHEN MADELINE STEPPED OUT into the reception area, she was an entirely different person, thoroughly composed, with her head held high. She figured they'd be waiting. Behind potted ferns, behind desks and partitions—to see just what sort of mincemeat the boss had made of this insubordinate. Let them wonder....

"Oh, Madeline," Sue sang out from her desk. "I have something for you."

Madeline strolled serenely across the carpet, swinging her bag at her side. The boss's warning must have really sent them scattering, for she and Sue were the only ones in the room, aside from the tall, thin, silver-haired gentleman in a brown suit entering with a coat draped over his arm. Bunch of groveling Creative Works cowards. Trey Turner's bark would never send her running for cover!

"You're Madeline?" The man in the brown suit had followed her to Sue's desk. And unlike Trey, he was openly glad to see her, as though they were dear old friends. Her mind raced as she scrutinized him. Late fifties. Graceful masculinity. Nice head of hair. As he took her hands in his, his sleeves rode up and she spotted an elegant gold timepiece on his left wrist. Monied good taste, right down to his Rolex. A date of Joanna's, perhaps? Just her mother's type—a strong male with old-world graces and a bit of coin to spend on dinner.

"Well, hello. How are you?" she improvised gaily.

"So you recognize me, eh?" His distinguished profile lit up. "I imagine Trey gave you a description."

Trey? Madeline slanted a wary look at Sue. The receptionist was truly petrified about something. She was pinching Madeline's final paycheck between purple fingers.

"Yes, this has to be Mr. Swain," Sue trilled on a false note. "Welcome to the New York offices of Creative Works, sir. We're honored that you could visit."

"Love New York," Harvey Swain enthused fluidly. "Greatest restaurants on earth. Don't you agree, Madeline?"

"I certainly do," she said with a huge smile. He was a nice man. How'd he ever end up in Trey's clutches?

"I can't tell you how anxious I've been to meet Trey's wife," he confided with pleasure. "You sounded too good to be true, from your faxes. But now that I see you in person, I believe each and every word."

Why had the jerk shown this man her faxes? He was obviously some client from California. "I'm Just Like a Wife," she declared, "as guaranteed."

Her statement brought a smooth laugh from Swain. "I imagine you are, m'dear. With a sense of humor to temper that hard-driven husband of yours. I feel a wife should complement her husband, don't you? Fill in those weak spots he has, round him off like a sturdy oak full of leaves. Makes a good executive a great one. My late wife undoubtedly made me a better man."

"It shows, Mr. Swain," she assured him, plucking her check from Sue's fingertips.

"Call me Swain, dear. Trey should've told you to."

"Why, even he wants me to call him Mr. Turner," she informed him evenly, tucking the check away in her purse. The cheapskate hadn't given her a penny of severance. Her hatred for him grew with every passing second!

"Our Madeline is such a kidder," Sue broke in with a laugh.

Our who? Madeline gaped at the other woman. What was going on here with Swain? And why on earth would Trey discuss her with this man in the first place? This setup had a fishy smell. . . .

"Madeline, don't forget that you have places to go and people to see," Sue urged with a pleading look in her eyes.

Unfortunately, she really did have to hustle. Vic was painting her today. Too bad. This was getting real good. "Nice meeting you, Swain," she said, giving his arm a pat.

"Until later," Swain intoned with a sure nod. "If Trey hasn't made plans, we'll do so for him."

Sue was up on her feet, leaning over her desk with a feverish look. "I believe that Mr. Turner has everything mapped out," she babbled.

It wasn't until Madeline was on the elevator that she remembered Operation Matrimony. Everybody was on alert for it—except for poor Sue Parker it seemed! Madeline suspected that the receptionist had revealed her identity out of turn, before scoping the office for the expected Mr. Swain. It would be bad for her, with Five's attitude on insubordination and all. Yes, the whole scene added up only one way. That buzzard had told his client that Madeline was his real wife! Swain obviously was gung ho on marriage. And rather than lose the deal, Five was pretending to be the well-rounded executive with the little woman at his side.

Madeline was grinning again as she stepped onto Fifth Avenue. Maybe her job wasn't lost yet. From the looks of it, no man had ever needed a wife more in his life than this confirmed bachelor.

"QUIT FIDGETING, MADDY," Vic chided, from his position at the easel. "Profiles are difficult enough without movement."

"Sorry, Vic. But this thing with Five... An hour later and I'm still steaming!"

The scruffy-looking man behind the easel made a growling noise as he jabbed his flat bristle brush into a dab of burnt umber oil on his palette. "Wash him clear of your mind. There are new lines around your mouth and eyes. Wicked little lines that detract from this celebration of innocence."

Dressed in her aqua linen skirt, and the white blouse she kept at Vic's specifically for the portrait, she struggled to remain still in the wooden chair, attempting to focus over Vic's shoulder at the mural on the wall. Her innocence concerning life's dirty dealing was long gone, despite Vic's pure vision for the canvas, but at least she could deliver a little serenity. The portrait was to be a Christmas gift for her mother.

Vic smiled in encouragement. "All you have to do now, love, is play the waiting game. No wife on earth has ever been in a better bargaining position than you are right now."

Madeline wasn't patient by nature, but she was inclined to agree with Vic's assertion. He had confirmed her suspicions about Trey's scheme to claim her as his wife for Swain's benefit. But Vic had also managed to give Trey's position an unexpectedly human slant. Swain's policy about married executives was narrow-minded by today's attitudes. And Trey was a superb adman who would do well by Swain, once given the account. Vic also confessed to having his own vested interest. Trey was planning to hire him to do some free-lance artwork for the campaign.

Though busting Trey—the way he'd busted her—would've been a treat to savor, Madeline realized that innocent people would no doubt be hurt. Yes, she would keep his little secret for him, if he asked her nicely.

Given the right incentive, even the feisty Madeline could do as she was told. Job reinstatement seemed fair. She wanted to be Trey's hired wife again, with permission to use his apartment on Fridays when he was out of town. Nothing less would do. After all, she could replace him a hundred times over without the Friday-night bonus. Couldn't she?

Madeline tingled uncomfortably as she thought back to how attracted she'd been to Trey down in the grill. He'd seemed so vulnerable seated opposite her in the booth, trying to pick her up with his boyish charm, fielding her verbal slings with good-humored prowess. But he was a totally different man in the office, so unrelenting and steely. His sensuality was the only thing that seemed to link the two separate personalities together. What that man did for a crisp white dress shirt was remarkable....

"Hmm, if you were thinking of me with that look on your face, I'd be tempted to marry you myself," Vic remarked with a glint in his eye.

"I was just thinking how complex Trey Turner is," she said calmly, attempting to battle the blush rising from her neck. "After working for him for nearly two months, handling everything from his personal calendar to his Jockey shorts, I figured I could've picked him out of a crowded room wearing a blindfold!"

Vic released a fleeting sigh. "I didn't think you were thinking of me."

"It's horrible to discover that I didn't recognize one of my own husbands, with all that evidence staring me right in the face."

"Hindsight is always clearer," Vic soothed.

"Adding insult to injury, he is not the prototype husband at all, is he?"

"Huh?"

"You know what I mean. He seemed like a heck of a good catch from afar."

Vic's fleshy jaw dropped. "For real?"

"Sure, for real. Not that I'd ever get romantically involved with one of my husbands," she promptly assured him.

"No, no, never."

"But as I searched for Mr. Right, using his place as my home base, I was on the lookout for the sort of man I believed Turner to be. Understand?"

"Well..."

"No, I'm asking too much of you. It's so deeply personal. He was my favorite husband, you know. Gallant and hardworking. So concerned about his mother's birthday, for instance. But this is the same man who demanded his key back. Who shoved his palm right under my nose."

"Who shared his dinner with you."

"Who offered me a pickle, then acted surprised when I took it! I don't even like pickles, but I took one just to show him. See what I mean about the inconsistencies, Vic? The guy is totally irritating, hopelessly frustrating."

"Sounds kind of . . . exciting."

"He fooled me all the way, with his polite communications, his tidy habits. He's the kind of husband who wouldn't bother me by beeper like some of them do."

Her pager began to sound off moments later, just as Vic again attempted to put his brush to canvas. Madeline lunged for her purse and dug for the small black box.

"It's him!" she squealed in schoolgirl delight, recognizing Trey's number on the digital display. "His direct line at the office."

Vic threw his arms into the air with a slightly mocking "Hallelujah!"

Madeline darted for the phone on Vic's desk, then froze with receiver in hand. "What am I doing? I don't even know what to say!"

Vic set his palette down on the worktable. "Settle down, babe. Take a deep breath. You're in the driver's seat this round. Swain has placed your face with your faxes and Trey has no choice but do a deal on bended knee."

With a bob of her head, Madeline punched in the number. "Hello. Yes, it's me, Madeline." Vic nodded in encouragement as her tone oozed menthol. "I'd like to talk to you, but Vic's painting my portrait right now."

Vic gave her the thumbs-up signal as he went about cleaning up for the day. "Over here? Now? I don't think—" With a gasp, she hung up the phone. "He's on his way over. The nerve!" She whirled toward her purse. "Guess I'll just go freshen up."

"You were fresh enough for the sitting," he protested.

"You have a way of smoothing over the spots a husband's eye wouldn't miss." She gave him a wink, zooming into the bathroom.

"If things get sticky, just follow my lead," Vic called after her.

Madeline peered out into the hallway, jabbing her brush at him. "But you said he'd be on his knees."

"Crawling will be a last resort. He'll come in swinging, hoping to regain leverage."

"Oh . . ." The news brought a trace of anxiety to her tone. She gulped a little, taking a couple of tentative steps back down the hallway. For the first time since junior high, Madeline found herself unnerved over a face-off with a male. She bit her lip and fumed in self-disgust. There was nothing to fret about. She'd inherited all the right stuff for a healthy man-woman encounter: her mother's flirtatious flair and Granny Dot's forthright nature. In general, she handled men remarkably well—the whole Clancy clan said so. Not just any woman could juggle five husbands with diplomatic skill by day, then sift through potential suitors with grace and good cheer by night.

So why was this anachronistic workaholic executive getting under her skin? No logical explanation came to mind.

"You're growing pale," Vic observed in a worried voice.

"That's absurd!"

"Hey, I'm the master of bravado," he scolded. "I know what I see. You're red, you're white—now red again." Before she could offer a rebuttal, he went on. "Trey is just a regular guy underneath his high-powered demeanor. True, he can seem one-dimensional and unrelenting. And he does think money can buy most anything, and that a stern policy keeps his employees in line—"

"Oh, jeez, Vic! The heartless dope isn't worth my time. And time is the one thing I have precious little of to waste these days."

"He's worth it, Maddy. He doesn't completely understand it yet, but he needs you desperately."

"Guys like Turner run on automatic pilot well into their forties. Then, as they approach middle age, they look back, aghast, wondering why they're all alone on Thanksgiving. I'll bet you he's planning to work through the holiday weekend."

"It's a bet I wouldn't touch," Vic confessed. "But I'm begging you to talk to him, give him a chance. Trey is the sort of pal men appreciate more readily—athletic, amusing, dependable. He's helped me out of dozens of jams over the past few years, showing the sort of good sense that he's so lacking in his own personal decisions. I'd just like to return the favor. He's drowning in his own dull routine and you're just the woman to revive him."

A fierce pounding on the apartment door interrupted them.

Vic crossed the living room, pausing to give her a bolstering smile. "Just remember, everything has a price tag to him. The more he pays, the better he feels."

"I don't want his money!"

"You might have to take some of it to get your job back."

Madeline shook her head in bewilderment. "Won't he just give me my job back?"

Vic paused with his hand on the safety chain. "He's pretty cautious with his employee relations. Whatever happens, follow my lead."

"Just couldn't resist turning the screw, could you, Mad?" Trey charged through the door, nearly plowing over his pudgy friend. He skidded to a stop before his startled ex-wife.

She looked up into his fiercely drawn features, down his heaving chest to the tips of his black leather shoes. He was standing toe-to-toe with her stocking feet. So close that her nose was almost buried in the knot of his striped tie. Vic obviously knew this man far better than she; he had entered swinging for all he was worth. Genuflecting seemed the farthest thing from his mind. But she wouldn't show a hint of uncertainty. A Clancy always stood firm, no matter what sort of storm swirled round.

"What are you talking about?" she demanded in a huff, tapping her toe against his wing-tipped one.

"Don't play coy with me. You were so bitter about being fired that you cozied up to Swain in revenge."

Madeline's mouth dropped open in amazement. "I didn't. I wouldn't."

"She couldn't," Vic put in adamantly.

"Shut up, Vic," Trey snapped, his eyes never leaving hers. "You told him you were my wife, Madeline."

"No, Trey. *You* told him I was your wife. I innocently made a remark about my company, Just Like a Wife." When she saw him wince, she knew reality was sinking in beneath his thunderous fury. Sue Parker had a part in the flub-up as well, but if Madeline could spare the poor woman her job along with her own, she would—by turning the screws on the real culprit in this whole affair. "Face it, Five, you tried to pull a fast one with Mr. Swain and he caught you at it."

The following silence was deafening. Trey was absolutely smoldering, with nowhere to place the blame.

"There must be a way we can patch this up to everyone's satisfaction," Vic casually suggested, wandering closer to the dueling pair.

"You two are in cahoots all the way, aren't you?" Trey accused, spinning around so fast that Madeline nearly toppled over.

Vic took up the slack, his stubbled face pleasant. "We're both on your side, Trey. Though I do have my own self-interest, of course. I'm behind on my alimony and desperately need the free-lance work on Swain's account."

"I didn't know you'd been married, Vic," Madeline blurted curiously.

"Four times." Trey snorted in disgust. "I wouldn't take too much advice from this revolving-door Romeo if I were you."

"Call me a romantic," Vic murmured, keeping his sense of humor. "When I fall in love, I like to tie the knot."

Trey scowled at his friend. "A failed fling is bad enough. But to endure the ache of divorce over and over again . . . It's not worth the plunge."

"But to never try," Vic scoffed, "to never legally commit, is worse! Maybe I go overboard with my marriages, but at least I've had my share of poignancy, of depth. It's made me an intuitive artist."

"The last one was a stripper from Nevada, Victor! She married you for money and you're still paying up. If a man stays single, he doesn't end up in dire straits when a relationship fizzles."

"You always put a price tag on everything," Vic shot back.

"Enough!" Madeline erupted, causing them to whirl on her in surprise. "I don't know which of you is more off the beam with your radical stands. I happen to have my own marriage plan. It falls somewhere between the two of yours, and it suits me fine."

Trey cocked a brow in query. "Honed it down, have you?"

"It's the simplest plan, really, as old as time—one man, a few kids, forever and ever."

The vision of coming home to Madeline every night sent a warm tingle through Trey's limbs. Settling back on a sofa before a crackling fire. Sipping martinis. Mulling over the day's events. Only to have her blasted beeper begin to *beep-beep-beep!*

She'd taken a step closer, her eyes sparkling with hope and determination.

What the hell was she going to ask of him? Do to him? It took his last reserve of courage to ask.

"All I want to do is start anew with you, Trey," she replied with a smile. "If you reinstate me, I'll be more than happy to play the happy homemaker during Swain's visit. We'll overlook this mishap, just go on as we were."

Her answer left him strangely aggravated. But was there anything she could've said that would have satisfied him? Probably not. He didn't know what to do with the emotions she evoked in him, or with the void her dismissal was bound to cause. But he shook his dark head vehemently under her anticipatory look. "No, no, I just can't see clear to going back to square one, allowing you to use my home as some sort of a nightcap central."

Her cry of dismay pierced the room. Vic held up a warning hand behind Trey's back, which she attempted to take to heart. "Okay," she said on a calmer note, "I'm willing to bargain. I'll never again allow a date to step over your threshold. How does that sound?"

Trey waved a hand in disgust.

"Okay, then. I'll meet them and leave them down in the grill." She clasped her hands together, her eyes full of yearning. "Oh, please, just let me sleep in your bed again."

The request left him speechless. Coming from a harder, more experienced woman, it would've instantly brought the cynical slash of a smile to his face. But in Mad's case he knew better, knew that nothing was ever as it appeared on the surface. The words, though blatant, were liquid honey from her mouth— sweet, innocent, genuine. Yet there was a sensuality in her eyes. A liquid-silver stirring that sent electric shocks through his body. His heart and loins were alive all at once. This feminine powerhouse was so endearing under all her bravado, and at the same time seductive.

A temptress in training. A half-open rosebud.

As though on autopilot, he raised a finger to her velvety cheek. She inhaled sharply at his stroke, as though suffocating. For a long, breathless moment they stared deeply into each other's eyes. And shared a startling realization. Trey wanted to open her petals, watch her bloom in his arms.

Madeline was awestruck by the intensity of the message. How could he be contemplating that sort of move now, in the center of this controversial storm? Perhaps it was an encouraging sign, that this adman of steel didn't bury all his feelings from nine to five as she'd earlier assumed. But where to take it. Did she want the man or the job? Once she took the man, she would no longer qualify for the platonic-wife position.

And just what was he offering? Why, he'd just denounced marriage. She'd like to think that the husband of her dreams would at the very least be of a marrying mind. As disappointing as it was, it appeared that Trey's apartment and the opportunities it offered seemed far more promising than the invitation in his eyes.

"Don't you know how dangerous it is to scour the city for a husband?" he broke into her thoughts to inquire.

"I'm always careful," she returned flatly. The message was received and understood, slicing right through the sizzle. Feeling more sure of herself, Madeline continued. "Look, Trey, if you weren't planning to hire me back, just what do you want?"

"I want you to play the role of my wife. Just for to-night. For Swain's sake."

"That's all?" she cried indignantly. "You zoomed over here to offer me a bit part?"

"Lead role," he corrected calmly. "Can't imagine you ever playing less to any man. You certainly have Swain hypnotized," he hastily clarified, feeling that his desires were already putting him at a distinct disadvantage. He'd never had trouble enforcing his strict employee policies before.

"I don't think my personality has much to do with this at all," she declared bluntly, folding her arms across her chest. "I think you're stuck with me because Swain has placed my face. Vic has already confirmed a lot of my suspicions," she put in when he seemed poised to object. "You've been passing me off as your long-distance wife for a while now, intending to keep me out of the way while you closed the deal."

"Right on all counts," he said, flaring, unable to keep his temper in check. "Swain finds you utterly—utterly—"

"Exciting," Vic mumbled behind a cough.

"Go back to your coloring books," Trey told him crossly.

"I was coloring her," Vic complained, gesturing to Madeline, "before you beeped in and spoiled things."

Trey spared a harried glance at the watch beneath his suit sleeve. "Time is ticking. I need an answer, Mad. Do you want the job?"

Madeline's gaze strayed to Vic, who had wandered over to the window. "Nothing wrong with a little free-lance work," Vic murmured, tapping a finger on the sill. "Just to stay in the game."

Madeline understood. She'd lose Trey and his apartment completely if she didn't play ball. "Can't say I'm thrilled with the terms...."

"The fee is the only question left," Trey persisted impatiently.

The artist raised three fingers behind Trey's back.

"Three," she blurted out.

"Three hundred?"

"Well...yeah," she affirmed when Vic nodded cooly.

Trey caught on to the silent communication and spun to confront his neighbor. "What kind of squeeze operation is this?"

Vic shot him a doleful look. "It's just her weekly wage, Trey."

"She's not doing her weekly duties."

"Put me back on the payroll and I'll do tonight for free," she offered, now in total harmony with Vic's strategy.

"Cheaper to keep her, Trey," Vic chimed in.

Trey's head bobbed, strands of brown hair falling over his forehead. "Not on your life. I will not see my New York haven turned into a bachelorette headquarters." He dug into his wallet and extracted three hundred-dollar bills. And to think that on the way over he'd lamented not breaking one of them for this payment! This novice operator was jerking him around like a puppet. But it would just be for one more night. One last night of Madness.

Madeline stared at the money as Trey pressed it into her palm. "So what's next?"

"It's crash-course time. I need lots of information—about you, your family. Personal things a husband would know. And you'll need something to wear.

Something on the conservative side, yet youthful. Nothing like that slinky red number," he cautioned with the shake of a finger.

"I don't own an executive-wife's outfit," she scoffed.

"Of course you don't," he said in a matter-of-fact way that rankled her.

"Just what do you mean?"

"I mean, when you dress up for dinner in the city, you're out to infatuate." When she opened her mouth to protest, he went on. "Don't try to deny it! That red dress is a seductive flag. I want Swain's eyes to stay above the shoulders." He took a deep, disgusted breath. "Don't argue every point here. Just go out and buy something suitable. You've got all afternoon."

Madeline gasped, slapping her hands to her cheeks. "I can't possibly give you the rest of the day! I have four other husbands to contend with back home. My schedule is impossible, what with Thanksgiving and all. Everything is topsy-turvy back in Tuckahoe. I'm expected right after lunch."

Trey didn't deny the territorial surge of emotion running through his veins this time, as he had when learning of Vic's friendship with Mad. When he paid for something, or someone, he was quite comfortable making demands. He seized her arms, giving her a gentle, impatient shake. "I expect you to jump whole-heartedly into this role. You are Mrs. James Turner III, bought and paid for until midnight tonight. Those are my terms. Nonnegotiable."

A secret feminine place deep inside Madeline tingled a bit at his possessive declaration. It was no wonder this man was a successful power player. He fit the mold perfectly with his dark good looks, his sure, modulated tone, his eyes gleaming with determination. But his husbandly attitude was a miracle of naiveté. Yes, Trey Turner joined the rest of the human race, with his own unique frailties. This man was afraid to express his needs unless he was picking up the tab! That was what Vic had been trying to tell her. Amidst Trey's many wonderful qualities dwelled a deep-seated fear of . . . what? Personal rejection? Her heart went out to him, even though she was nearly irritated enough to chase him with a rolling pin.

Madeline laid the bills on Vic's old, scarred desk.

"What the hell!" Trey roared in surprise. "Are you quitting on me?"

It took all her self-control not to grin into his horrified face. She'd never been so desired by a husband. "I simply have to make some calls, Trey. Rearrange my schedule." She picked up the cordless phone and her heavy leather sack. "This deal lasts till midnight, right?"

"Right."

"Then I will be free to return to Tuckahoe?"

Trey held up a palm. "Absolutely. I'll drive you home myself."

She headed for the apartment's only bedroom and shut the door behind her.

Trey raked his hair with shaky fingers. "Think she'll do it, Vic?"

Vic nodded, giving him an encouraging slap on the back. "It'll be fine."

In silent agreement they wandered quietly toward the chirping voice muffled by the door. They listened for a while, exchanging awestruck looks over seemingly intricate plans being made and remade. For the next twenty minutes, Madeline talked to merchants, home base, secretaries and husbands. Most of all husbands.

Trey couldn't suppress the feelings of envy as he listened to her cajole and console numbers One through Four, her tone and mood a virtual panoply in variety. On a rational plane, it only proved to him that he was not the special husband of her life, as he'd fancied himself to be over the past several weeks. She was a real pro who delivered consistent satisfaction, which, as a fellow entrepreneur, he could easily admire. But his male pride was taking a beating. He had the feeling that if all five of her husbands ever ended up in a room together, vying for her attention, there'd be fisticuffs for sure!

Trey took a couple of steps back, shaking his head in disbelief. "How can she handle it all, Vic?"

Vic wiped his face with his hand to cover a smirk. "Dynamite lady."

"Any employee worth having is bound to be in demand," Trey reasoned, reaching back into his suit jacket pocket for his wallet. "Even a temporary one."

"What are you doing?" Vic asked in shock.

"Sweetening the kitty, of course."

"You don't have to do that, Trey!"

"I can't stand out here any longer," Trey confided bleakly, "wondering...."

It saddened and frustrated Vic to see his friend lean so heavily on the dollar for results. And it was partially his fault this time. He'd started this free-lance wife-for-the-night business himself, hoping to show Trey that some things couldn't be paid for so easily. But the nervous entrepreneur had called his bluff and met their price. Trey was hiding behind a wall of cash, and it was killing his love life. He was just too busy and too damn rich to reach people on a basic human level.

Trey extracted another hundred-dollar bill and crouched down to slip it halfway under the bedroom door. Within seconds it disappeared inside. Madeline soon appeared, meeting Trey's hopeful look with a twinkle.

"Well, Mad?"

"You've got yourself a wife, Five. To have and to hold until the clock strikes twelve."

6

LATER THAT EVENING Trey again found himself listening to Madeline through a closed door. This time she was speaking for his benefit, from his bedroom.

"Time is of the essence, Mad," he prompted, his hand squeezing the knob. "Harvey Swain will be here soon."

"A quick change, and I'll be out."

"Need anything?"

"No, I'm the wife who knows where everything is, remember?"

How true. If he had a skeleton in the closet, she'd know. But he had the feeling that if she found one, she'd just dust it and go on to the next task. Trust. It all narrowed down to trust. He paced around, rubbing his knuckles against his teeth. He sure was putting his trust in her tonight. But judging from her performance record, she could handle it. She seemed ethical enough to deliver what he'd paid for. Though he would never again trust her alone with his apartment, he was quite confident he could manipulate her behavior in a controlled situation.

Admittedly, there was one weak link in tonight's chain of deception: Mad knew him a whole lot better than he knew her. They'd started some of the preliminary groundwork—names and ages of the Clancys under her roof, personal background on her schooling, preferences, friends. Then she'd taken a look at the

clock and declared that she had to get ready. She left
Trey standing stock-still in shock in the center of his
own living room, with a mental list of half-answered
questions and a heart hungry for her attention. He'd
tried to detain her, but she shut the door in his face with
a huff. So, on second thought, maybe controlling her
behavior wasn't such a sure thing, after all. . . .

As the minutes ticked by, Trey tried to shake off the
feeling that his power as employer in this circumstance
was on a sliding scale. He was accustomed to sitting
atop the heap, doling out fair but dictatorial direction
to his staffers. With Mad he seemed to be on a teeter-
totter. Sometimes she was on top, other times he was,
and the fall to the ground each and every time sent his
guts up into his throat.

An attitude adjustment was in order. Just who would
be making it would no doubt be a duel until the stroke
of midnight.

"Can I answer any last questions?" she called suddenly from behind the bedroom door.

"Yes! Yes, you can!" His heels pounded across the
living room carpet and down the short hallway, his
heart thumping in gratitude. He knew, of course. Knew
she was again yanking him back into her web. The
muffled voice belonged to the efficient Just Like a Wife,
the nurturing caregiver he'd grown to rely upon so
heavily. Forgotten was her sniff of protest when he'd
tried to postpone her dressing ritual with the snag of a
wrist and a growl of desperation.

"Both your grandmother and mother are widows,
right?" he hastily reiterated. "Well, fill in the blanks
there."

"My grandfather, Charles Clancy, died ten years ago. Lung cancer. Granny Dot's been with us ever since. My dad, Robert, died fourteen months ago. Heart attack. Very unexpected, very tough. My mom, Joanna, is what you might call a dependent housewife. She's never held a job outside the home and has no interest in doing so."

"So she's your inspiration in the domestic department."

Lilting laughter reached him through the door. "No. Our house was pandemonium until Granny Dot moved in. She's the Clancy cornerstone, the epitome of order and practicality. She's never held an outside job, either. Came straight from the farm to us."

Trey stroked his chin in bemusement. No obvious mentor to explain the multifaceted Madeline-Mad, superwife to five men and sassy diva to blind dates.

"Mom's a romantic with a wildly creative mind," Madeline went on to explain. "The mother on the block with the bottomless pitcher of lemonade, who plays kickball with the kids. The scout den leader who's never at a loss for craft-project ideas."

"Sounds financially impossible," the businessman in him blurted out.

There was silence on the other side of the door, then, in an odd tone, she mentioned that Robert Clancy had had the foresight to buy life insurance.

Trey sighed deeply. Leave it to him to cut right to dollars and cents. She hadn't liked the question. He'd try to be more tactful. "Must be tough, with the boys still being so young."

"We manage," she returned spunkily. "A Clancy never panders for pity."

Trey rolled his eyes toward the ceiling. "Heaven forbid."

"Your mother sounds nice," she ventured. "Sent me a charming thank-you note for arranging her birthday party."

"Yeah. She's the sweet, adorable type."

"Widow?"

"Divorcée. Three times over. My father was her first husband. He disappeared during my toddler years. She was soon hitched to number two. That union lasted through my teens. She was single for quite a while afterward."

"And what of the third one?"

"He was a stage actor twenty years her junior—a nine-month mistake. I moved her to California for a fresh start after that fiasco."

"Oh."

"Oh?" Trey repeated on the upshot.

Mad opened the door a crack, hastily sashing his terry robe around her middle. "You got a problem with oh?"

"No."

She nodded. "Good."

He put a palm on the door as she was about to close it again in his face. "Look, I know what you're insinuating. That I'm opposed to marriage because of my mother's failures—"

"I didn't say that!"

"One 'oh' from you speaks volumes."

She sighed. "Okay. So you caught me. I do think we're all influenced by our upbringing. My folks made the most of their union. It was a pleasure watching them love each other. Maybe this talk will help you understand my point of view, Trey," she ventured on a soft, hopeful note. "Why I want a genuine husband of my own."

Internal alarms jangled from his head to his toes as Trey felt the pull of her psyche, drawing him into deep waters he rarely entered. The whole situation was painfully laughable. Inside his bedroom stood the most intriguing, alluring woman he'd ever met, and here he stood, on the opposite side of the door. Just as he stood on the opposite side of some personality issues. This chick had incredible nerve, juggling five men while hunting for a real husband in her spare time. What sort of dude would settle for a slice of her attention on the wrong side of the door? But what red-blooded male could help but wonder what it would be like to plumb her depths completely, be the man of her dreams?

"Just what sort of man would fit the bill?" he found himself asking.

"An adventuresome man who is up to an equal partnership," she promptly replied, her eyes shimmering with mischief and feminine secrets. "One who will understand my flights, my ambitions. Life is an open door to me. The possibilities are endless."

His heart skipped a beat. Even with her face stripped of makeup, it had a luminous glow. To think he'd assumed Ms. Clancy to be the plain, safe type! But only because she was so good at her job. It still seemed damn near impossible to believe that a seductive superwife could exist outside an executive's fantasies. But the proof stood before him. In the flesh. Lean, curvacious. Nearly nude beneath his gaping robe, save for her stockinged legs....

To his own amazement, the separate Mad Madeline personalities began for the very first time to merge in his mind—superimposed over an erotic outfit of stockings, heels and sheer apron. His blood heated at the graphic image. He savored it for a long luscious moment, adding a ruffled hemline to the apron just below the curve of her hip.... With a sharp swing back to reason, he fought to suppress the picture, to drive it back to the corner of his brain where all his ideas hatched. He couldn't afford to stand here shuddering like a sixteen-year-old looking at *Playboy* magazine! It was the curse—and blessing—of having a wild imagination. His advertising mind frequently illustrated things symbolically. It was part of his job—a reflexive act. Behavior he couldn't afford tonight with Swain on the string.

"Well, you sure have the experience to do the marriage right," he eventually remarked thickly, leaning against the doorjamb as he gathered his wits.

"What?" Her delicate brows rose a mile.

"I mean it in the nicest way," he hastened to add. "Any woman who can keep five bachelors straightened out is a miracle on heels."

"Why, thank you," she accepted graciously. "Who knows, maybe one day you'll even see the light. My mother, at forty-nine, would like to marry again."

Tension tightened Trey's jaws once again. "So would mine, at the age of fifty-nine! And it's the last thing she needs!"

With a grunt of disgust she again tried to heave the door shut. This time he let her.

When Madeline emerged from the bedroom a short time later, masculine laughter reached her ears. The two men, dressed in dark suits, were standing at the window facing Riverside Drive as she entered the living room.

"Madeline!" Harvey Swain greeted her, his distinguished features alight. "The view of the Hudson River is a scene second only to you!"

Madeline strolled forward to offer her hand, aware that Trey was beaming beside Swain. She deserved his approval. She'd gone to great pains to find just the right outfit for her executive-wife role—a double-breasted coatdress of navy rayon. Conservative, yet curve friendly. She'd chosen to wear her golden, orange-tinged hair loose, curled below the shoulders in a subdued page boy. Overall, a soft yet sophisticated look.

"Good evening, Mr. Swain," she murmured charmingly. "How lovely of you to treat us to dinner."

"My pleasure." Harvey Swain bowed slightly. "Trey was just treating me to some of his specialty wine. He won't tell me exactly what kind it is, however...."

Can't tell you, Swain, Madeline thought with a tight-lipped look. It was the wine she supplied to all her husbands, one of the perks allowed those who kept her on the payroll as Just Like a Wife! The notion that he was calling it his own seemed out of line, considering that he'd dismissed her. The wine should be hers again by default.

As should the vase of freshly arranged flowers on the table. Both Trey and Swain had plucked carnations from it for their lapels. Furthermore, Trey had pulled out his engagement calendar, the small looseleaf booklet Madeline supplied to all her husbands for their personal obligations and dutifully kept up-to-date. He was currently running his finger over her neatly written notations, leaving the impression that the book was frequently conferred over by husband and wife.

Trey was certainly offering Swain the hospitality of the house. The house she'd made a home. So the damn fool didn't think he needed her anymore! His life wasn't going to run far on automatic pilot. The wine would dry up, the flowers would wilt and the calender would go blank on the first of December. Somehow the idea of Trey hanging on to the edge of bachelorhood oblivion by his fingernails brought a dazzle to her smile.

Until he held up her white half-slip. The one she'd worn underneath her suit this morning. Right before their eyes he dug it out from between the sofa cushions and passed it to her with a sheepish look.

Her eyes widened; her voice squeaked. "What the—"

Trey cut her short with a small cough. "I believe you overlooked this, honey."

And you're a dead man, dear. She accepted the scrap of lacy nylon, hiding her slitted look from Swain behind a curtain of hair. Sometime, presumably while she was showering, he'd dug through her things and brought the slip out for this cozy display! "I'll just get my purse," she said lightly.

"I'll confirm our reservations," Swain announced, striding toward the phone on the coffee table. "I hope the Four Seasons suits you...."

Madeline sent the slip sailing toward the bed, then turned sharply when she realized Trey had followed her into the bedroom.

"You aren't bringing along that huge sack of wifely tools of the trade, are you?" he demanded in an urgent whisper.

"No!" she retorted, picking up the new, black satin evening bag from the dresser.

"Are you mad?" he asked in obvious surprise.

"You mean angry mad or nutty mad?" she shot back furiously, parroting his own words of the other night.

"Look, I only did the slip thing because the place—" He lifted his hands in a helpless gesture. "You've got things looking so damn perfect around here, it seems artificial! You're simply too good to be true!" he added at her unwavering glare.

"Oh yeah?" she challenged, poking her finger to his chest. "Then why didn't you go for broke and hang your jocks on the lampshade?" She chuckled softly at his mortified look. "Maybe next time, eh?"

His look was thunderous. "There isn't going to be a next time, Mad."

"Then we'd better make the most of tonight," she snapped saucily to his back as he marched out the door.

It was advice she planned to follow. With sudden inspiration Madeline rummaged through her leather bag for her pager, slipping the small black gadget into her satin bag. She would most definitely make this a most memorable night for her former Number Five—torture the daylights out of him under the innocent eye of Harvey Swain. And there was absolutely nothing he could do but take the medicine. Yes, that slip over her slip was the last straw. His money compensated for only so much. If a man was going to drink her wine and snap off her carnations, he had better be a husband with a number. If he was going to display her underwear in public, he'd damn well better be a husband with a ring!

A ring? So what was Trey to her, anyway, she wondered. A potential suitor or an employer? At the moment, he seemed too damn infuriating to be either. Madeline didn't like the helpless feeling, the uncertainty of where they were headed. Suddenly the midnight hour seemed an eternity away.

THE FOUR SEASONS restaurant was a favorite of Madeline's, with its shimmering pool and notable artwork. Her father had proposed to her mother there years ago, making the place especially sentimental to all the Clancys. They still dined there when the budget allowed for dinner and a Broadway show. So naturally, when Trey gave her arm a warning squeeze inside the entrance while Swain was checking their coats, Madeline was incensed.

"What's the matter, Five. My slip showing again?"

"Ha ha."

"Or is it tucked away in your jacket pocket, just in case I seem a little too perfect here too?"

He draped his arm around the shoulders of her coatdress, his mouth grazing the curve of her ear. His voice was fluid, his breath warm as he spoke into her ear. "I'm not worried about perfection during this stage of the evening. Elegance, subdued grace—those are the things my imaginary wife would exhibit in this superdeluxe restaurant."

"You adman beast," she muttered between gritted teeth. "I got the meaning of your squeeze, all right. It was a warning, a reprimand, an expression of naked fear!"

"All that and more, Mad. Take forks, for instance. Do you know which fork to use when?"

"They're all good for a quick scratch on the back," she returned airily. "But the longer the tongs, the better, I guess."

With a furtive look toward the coat-check counter, he clucked in a low tone, "Now, for four hundred bucks, I deserve a little reassurance and cooperation. Our other meal out was indisputably casual, even for the grill."

"Why you—"

He cut short her indignant gasp by pressing a finger to her lips. "I simply want you to understand from the onset that this isn't the sort of place where food is served familystyle. Each person has his or her own plate and utensils. One doesn't reach a bangled arm across the table to grab another's goodies with greedy fingers."

Madeline flipped her hands for inspection. "I'm not wearing bangles tonight."

"Just keep your patties off my pickles!" he directed sternly.

"You've got a nerve, fancying yourself the Prof. Henry Higgins of Manhattan," she returned in a quiet huff. "Well, let me tell you, I'm no guttersnipe in need of direction. We Clancys do dine out on occasion—in Tuckahoe, and here at The Four Seasons." With a glance at the approaching Swain, she hastened to add, "No wife—hired or otherwise—wears her apron twenty-four hours a day!"

Visions of Mad in his dream-conjured apron danced in Trey's head as the maître d' showed them to their table. Usurped before the soup, and as randy as a sailor on leave. This woman had an incredible effect on him. Leaving him to quell both his temper and his desires.

How did they drift so far from the ultimate goal of charming his potential client?

Surely no husband on earth had ever felt as trapped in matrimony as he did right now. And he hadn't even gotten a honeymoon out of the deal!

Once food orders were given to the waiter and the trio had their drinks before them, Madeline sensed a feeling of expectation settle over the table. Harvey Swain was focusing on her in curious admiration, she noted, as though he was mentally preparing for small talk. He seemed relaxed and unassuming as he enjoyed his Scotch. Trey was taut as a bowstring beneath his tailored gray suit, and in an obvious effort to stay alert, was favoring ginger ale. Madeline was treading the moderate middle with a glass of white wine, something she'd become an expert at nursing during her date-waiting hours in the Skyline Grill.

She released a steadying breath as she responded to Swain's gaze with a smile. Most likely he considered this dinner little more than a formality, a chance to unwind and get to know his new advertising representative. Trey was absolutely certain that Swain was ready to sign, perhaps as soon as tomorrow morning. She would indeed keep up her part of the bargain, but Trey deserved to squirm, she reaffirmed to herself with mounting annoyance. Imagine, flying through life on a magic carpet made of dollar bills! Paving over the rough spots with a smattering of coin.

Despite Vic's insistence that there was a lot more to Trey than the ambitious wheeler-dealer, Madeline was still struggling with her doubts. On one level she seethed over his bossiness, his arrogance, his apparent blindness to the human equation. On another, deeper plane, however, she desperately wanted to believe there was a sensitive boy hidden away within the man, deprived of a secure upbringing, fearful of expressing his emotions. For, whatever his failings, Madeline found herself attracted to him. A Clancy was always in touch with every feeling and ready to spring into appropriate action. She wasn't about to back away from the fact that Trey, a.k.a. Five, fit the prototype of her Mr. Right in so many ways. Hadn't she been looking for a handsome, successful executive all along? The only way she could think of to cause him to erupt was to put him to a stress test. Churn up whatever lay beneath his urbane exterior.

"So, Madeline," Swain said, slicing into her thoughts, "perhaps you can expound on your life with this creative genius. As thorough and inventive as he is in business, he is personally obtuse."

Trey was quick on the uptake. "Cut me some slack, Swain," he pleaded with a chuckle. "I explained how Madeline and I eloped back in September. The ceremony was simple. Private."

"So how did you like that part of the country?" Swain asked her as he tamped tobacco into the bowl of his pipe.

"Well, the climate was . . ." She trailed off, her eyes wide as they locked in on Trey. He lifted his knife, then ever so casually tipped it in the direction of the flickering candle in the center of the table. "Lovely, but hot," she swiftly finished.

"Hot in the mountains?"

Swain asked the question with some surprise, but seemed far more intent on lighting his pipe and puffing it to life than anything else. It was Trey's look that was meeting hers head-on. It was positively lethal as he picked up his water glass for a significant sip. He'd been pointing the knife to her water, apparently. But he'd been way off the mark, from her point of view. Hah! To think this was the same man who'd fretted over *her* clumsiness with utensils!

"Now, dear," he began, his tone dripping with tolerance, "it may have been hot in the Vegas wedding chapel, but our cabin in Lake Tahoe was on the cooler side during the entire week."

Madeline fluttered her lashes as she reached over to grasp his fingers. "I guess the weather was the last thing on my mind," she cooed huskily, favoring Swain with a brief, pleading look. "I remember lots of heat. And we rarely left the cabin...."

Trey could feel a flush rising from his throat as he removed his hand from hers, taking another sip of water to justify the move. To his horror, his cheeks actually began to singe under her pouty, amorous look, as though she'd delivered an openhanded slap, or a caress.... Either way, he was imagining her touch—for the hundredth time since their initial encounter in the grill. He was now more than ready to admit he wanted physical contact with this mad maid of a phony wife. Perhaps he could be on top of her for once. Be in control just once!

The more he thought about it, the better it sounded. One bounce on his bed and he'd wipe the smirk from her full, painted lips. It would jump from her mouth to his with lightning speed.

Time passed slowly in Trey's mind as he measured it course by course, sentence by sentence. An aura of sexual tension, intermingled with Swain's fragrant pipe smoke and the outlandish lies, hovered over their table like a musky cloud. She felt it, too, with every bite. Every look. Spells of relief hit the bogus couple only during intermittent personal anecdotes from Swain. For a client interested in checking out his potential employee, he certainly did a lot of the talking. By the time dessert was upon them in the form of cake and coffee, Trey thought his nerves would snap in two.

"I understand all about the joys of matrimony," Swain was expounding as the waiter set his cheesecake before him. "Losing my wife a couple of years ago was a tragedy. Of course, my four children and my grandchildren have eased my pain considerably...."

It was Swain's hand Madeline reached out for this time. "A good marriage is life's greatest achievement," she murmured in all sincerity. "Why, my own mother, Joanna, is in your predicament. She lost my father after a long, satisfying marriage."

Swain's aristocratic features expressed genuine concern. "How long has she been a widow?"

"About fourteen months now."

"I hope she is managing."

"She copes. And still being quite the femme fatale, she dates. I hope she marries again one day. She so enjoys being a wife."

"How wonderful!" Swain turned to Trey with a furrowed gray brow. "You've told me so little about Madeline's family."

"Oh, darling!" It was Mad's turn to express endearing exasperation. "Considering what my family means to me—to us—I'd have expected you to go overboard!" She pierced a glossy cherry from her Black Forest cake with her fork and lifted it to her mouth.

"They are a most colorful bunch, Swain. You'd truly love them. Especially my mom. I just happen to have some photos in my wallet . . ."

"I certainly love Joanna," Trey chimed in heartily, watching Mad's tongue capture a smidgen of cherry glazing from the corner of her mouth as she passed some pictures to Swain. "We have a heck of a time playing canasta together, just the two of us."

Madeline bristled, fighting to swallow her temper along with the cherry. Logic ruled his remark innocent and harmless, one that need never be proven after he landed the account, but here he was, laying claim to not only her wine and her carnations, but the affections of her own mother! He had no right. If he wanted all that, he should've kept her on. Or turned her on! Not only had he dismissed her professionally, but sexually as well. She'd gone to so much trouble to look her best for him tonight. As a husband—phony or genuine—he should've said something appreciative.

"She is truly lovely!" Swain enthused. "And she's unattached, you say. . . ."

"Unattached but well taken care of," Trey assured him, dripping a bit of cream into his coffee. "Between Joanna, Madeline and my own mother, I'm always in one henhouse or another!"

Yeah, right. Madeline bit her lip to suppress a squeal. Here was a guy with no time for women! Sweet-tongued devil. With a vengeful surge she grabbed the sugar bowl. As Trey slowly stirred his cream-clouded coffee, she plunked sugar cubes into his cup, one, two, three.

"There you are, darling," she trilled. "Just the way you like it."

Trey grimaced, seeing no alternative but to taste the syrupy blend. Just the way he liked it? Mad across his lap for a sound paddling was how he'd like it!

"Too much sugar can give you high blood pressure," Swain cautioned, returning the pictures.

As Trey sought a new, neutral conversational route, a series of beeps erupted from Madeline's lap. His spine and smile stiffened simultaneously at the familiar sound. She couldn't! She wouldn't! She didn't despise him that much, did she?

"Oh, my." Madeline reached into her purse and switched off the pager. She then stood with an apologetic look. "If you'll excuse me for a moment or two..."

Swain half rose, dabbing his mouth with his napkin. "I imagined that to be a call for Trey."

"It's for me," she corrected him. "Trey can explain. I'll be right back."

Before Trey could stop her, Madeline was wending her way through the dining room. Never in his entire life had he been so tormented by a woman, so torn between strangulation and consummation.

When Madeline hung up the telephone near the powder room several minutes later, Trey was waiting right behind her. She whirled, emitting a small squeak of shock as her nose met against his striped navy tie. "What? Where?"

"Which one was it?" he asked through gritted teeth.

"Two. He couldn't find his metal detector—"

"Well, he can shove his metal detector..." Taking a steadying breath, Trey ever so surreptitiously crowded her up against the wall. "When I pay for something, I expect full satisfaction," he said quietly. "You were to leave those other husbands behind tonight. Yet you deliberately, mindfully—" he drew his curled hand to her face, skimming the length of her jawline— "disobeyed me. All over again. Again and again!"

Her knees were knocking under her coatdress with his every stroke, but Madeline kept her chin high and steady. "With your attitude, it's no wonder you're still single!" she hissed. "A wife to you would be nothing but another asset. Another tax deduction!"

"Ours has never been more than a business proposition, Ms. Clancy," he reminded her tersely, dropping his hand from her face.

Madeline nodded mutely, recognizing and sharing the doubt in his tone. Testing each other's limits right now seemed about as safe as dumping vials from an old chemistry set into a blender and pushing the Whip button.

"We'll be having one hell of a discussion later on," Trey vowed in a growl, his dark eyes drilling hers. "I want to know why you've been doing your level best to make an ass of me all evening long. But right now it's imperative that we get back to the table. I told Swain I was checking up on you."

"What sort of explanation did you give him?"

"None. I just spent my time lapping up that horrible sugared coffee. The beeper trick is all yours."

"But Swain—"

"For once don't argue," he cut in harshly. "Just think hard and fast. Come up with a good explanation for it."

"But Swain's coming out of the dining room right now, you idiot!" she whispered, peering over his arm. "I need time to think!"

Before Madeline could take another breath, Trey swept her into his arms for a kiss. She instantly took him up on the stalling tactic, wrapping her arms around his neck with feigned newlywed eagerness.

It was Trey's turn to deliver a surprise. Wedged between his solid length and the wall, Madeline soon found herself aware of the sinewy strength of his limbs, the force behind his embrace. She instinctively liquified against him as he kissed her hard, his hands splaying across her back. Her pulse was racing. Play-acting or reacting?

"Think," he urged against her mouth, before plunging his tongue between her lips.

He expected her to think under these conditions? For a workaholic executive, he delivered a doozy of a smooch. This guy sure hadn't been hiding behind a wall of paperwork his whole adult life. He'd most likely been exercising his lips from his playground days on!

When Swain cleared his throat for the second time, Trey pulled his mouth from hers, and set her back on the floor. No wonder she felt light-headed!

"I began to wonder..." Swain offered in gentlemanly tones. "Thought I'd follow up—"

"Everything is just fine," she blurted out breathlessly with a hand to her heart. "I have the pager for my family's sake," she rattled on to explain. "We are so close knit. And sometimes my mother needs me. But nothing on earth is wrong. She was just checking in, as she often does."

Trey shoved his hands in his pockets, turning to conceal a wince. On the lips of a lesser woman, the answer would've sounded patently false. But Swain was obviously swallowing it. Enamored as he was with Mad, he probably would've believed anything by now. She could've claimed to have been beeped by the president of the United States and gotten away with it.

"Glad all is well." Swain linked arms with Madeline, steering her back toward the dining room. "Shall we finish our dessert? I'm so anxious to hear more about your charming mother—and the others, of course."

Trey followed on their heels, his heart slamming against his rib cage. It had been close. And it wasn't the charade that had him shook up, but Madeline's effect on his senses. One kiss had rendered him nearly helpless. If Swain hadn't come along when he did . . . But he had come along, and Trey had managed to break away.

Still, it would be wise to keep in mind just how dangerous Madeline was to his status quo. One touch and she'd nearly stolen all reason away. With a firm nod, he decided that in future, a hands-off policy would be best. The midnight countdown was approaching. Down would come the curtain on this zany brush with matrimony.

7

"GOOD EVENING, Mr. and Mrs. Turner! So nice to see you this evening!"

Trey glared at the Skyline Grill's lanky, fair-haired bartender as he and Madeline slid onto the end stools near the lobby doorway.

"Knock it off, Eddie. We're alone."

Eddie rubbed a towel over the puddled bar, removing two empty glasses with practiced grace. "But you said you were going to bring the frozen-food king back here. You said you'd forgive me for the maid scam if I pretended this gorgeous creature was your real wife."

"Well, I guess we wore the king out at dinner," Trey grumbled. "He's probably in his jammies by now over at the Pierre."

Eddie's pale brows lifted. "Whew, fancy accommodations."

"He can afford it," Trey assured dryly. "Wined and dined us at the Four Seasons. Even insisted on paying our cab fare."

"An old-world gentleman all the way," Madeline chimed in.

"Sounds like a free ride for you, Trey," Gina teased, circling round beside Eddie.

"Not exactly," Trey objected through gritted teeth, thinking back on the four bills he'd sunk into his free-lance wife. All that cash should've guaranteed sterling behavior. Mad behavior was what he'd gotten instead. Totally, utterly mad. If nothing else, he would get an explanation. She owed him that much. And it was time to pay up!

"Can I get you kids martinis?" Eddie inquired.

"They'll be on me," Gina announced. "My way of making up for Friday night's spoof." The petite blonde could no longer suppress her giggles. "I still can't believe Vic had to tell you Madeline was your maid, Trey."

"I suppose it's the hottest news around the building," Trey muttered, raking a hand through his dark, cropped hair.

"Damn right," Eddie affirmed, setting cocktail napkins before them.

"No thanks," Madeline declined, absently fingering the small paper square. Before Trey could speak for himself, she added, "He'll have to pass, too. He still has to drive me back to Tuckahoe."

Trey nodded wearily.

"We could get going," she suggested, her bottom fidgeting on the smooth bar stool.

Trey instantly noted her discomfort. It was so deliciously gratifying that he decided to milk it to the max. He tapped his watch with a satisfied grunt. "It's only ten to twelve, Mad. You are bought and paid for until the stroke of the hour." His remark caused Eddie and Gina to exchange looks of wonder, but Trey was beyond caring what was on the Skyline grapevine. This was his last chance to clear the air. He surely couldn't interrogate her and drive at the same time. Primed for confrontation, he turned sideways on the stool, resting his forearm on the bar. "We are going to spend what's left on the meter discussing your disgraceful behavior!"

Madeline's profile twitched. Just a little bit. But when she turned to meet him squarely, her expression was keen and unwavering. "I was a most gracious hostess."

"But a most antagonistic wife!"

She grinned smugly. "Couldn't resist taking a few jabs at you, Five."

"Why?" he demanded with open sarcasm. "You feel underpaid? Working conditions at The Four Seasons unsatisfactory?"

Eddie and Gina followed their banter like spectators at a tennis match, their eyes shifting to one, then the other.

"No and no!" Madeline blurted, openly disgusted. "You just don't see anything, do you? It never was the money."

"But you took the money," he challenged in a surprised tone.

"Only because Vic said you wouldn't feel secure unless you paid big."

His face twisted in a scowl. "Always good to know one can count on a friend's discretion."

"He was only trying to help! And boy, does he know you inside out!"

Touché. Trey couldn't deny he preferred to settle things with a buck. For all the good it did him tonight. "We're veering off from the issue here," he pointed out persistently. "The question is simple. Why did you take on the role of my wife in seemingly good faith, then spend the entire evening turning the thumbscrews on me?"

"This is how it stacks up." She punctuated each word with a fingernail tap to the bar. "First you fire me for insubordination—"

"But you knew that ahead of time!"

"Yes. But you went ahead and took advantage of all the perks you were no longer entitled to," she complained in a fluster. "You had the absolute gall to pass off my wine as yours. To—to snap off carnations from my floral arrangements for your lapels. To stuff my half-slip—the very slip you fired me in—down the cushion of the sofa!"

"Why'd you do that, Trey?" Eddie asked in wonder, stepping even closer to the pair.

Trey gestured helplessly. "Because it seemed like a way to display intimacy."

"And to make me look like a messy housekeeper!" Madeline fumed to the couple.

"It never occurred to me that you'd be offended," he shot back hastily. "And the differences between your old job and your free-lance one seemed inconsequential."

Madeline gasped in dismay. "What a cop-out for a man who thinks in methodical business terms every second of the day! Who hammers out deals with razor-sharp precision. Who fired me over a little personal complaint. Suddenly things are murky? You just picked through the Madeline Clancy buffet tonight and took whatever perks worked best. He even pretended to love my mother," she informed the blond pair. "And she doesn't even like canasta!" This last statement was lost on them, but neither dared ask for details as she spun on the stool, back to Trey. "And the crowning jewel of the night is that I did my job flawlessly. Swain wanted to see you in a stable, loving environment, and I delivered, mister!"

"I say that you were paid for what you did," he maintained in livid bewilderment. "And you should've kept your petty pranks out of it."

"You are too involved in sticking a price tag on everything," she hurled back at him in return. "In never cutting slack when an employee like me doesn't measure up perfectly in your eyes. There was no harm whatsoever in me using your place for overnight stays. And had you kept me on, I would've done tonight for free." She sighed hard, easing off the stool. "And, as you're so dissatisfied with my performance, I'm giving you your money back!" She stood beside him, rooting with a jerky hand through her satin bag.

"Never mind," he said with a dismissive gesture. "You're . . . right when you say you did the job. Swain's snowed. That's what I paid you for."

She pulled out some folded bills and pressed them into his palm. "Here you go, big shot. As it's after midnight, I'd like to get my things from your apartment and go home to Tuckahoe, where men and women say what they mean and mean what they say!" On that note she marched off toward the door to the Towers lobby.

"The poor kid," Gina murmured with a wistful look after Madeline.

Trey had unfolded the four bills intending to stuff them in his wallet, when he noticed they weren't the hundreds he'd given her. "Hey, Mad! Hey, hold on there!" But Madeline kept moving. Right through the glass door. "Poor kid nothing," he squawked. "She's only returned three tens and a one. Made that big speech and coughed up a meager thirty-one bucks!"

As Trey bounced off the stool, Eddie set the phone atop the bar. "Shall I alert Vic again?"

Trey spun on him with a lethal look. "Stay clear. She's on her own this time!"

"I was thinking of backup for *you,* buddy," Eddie called after him with a chuckle.

Mad, of course, had no choice but to wait for him outside his locked apartment with toe-tapping impatience. To avoid a scene in the hallway, he quietly opened the door and ushered her inside. She raced for the bedroom and started throwing her belongings into her roomy leather sack.

He watched her progress dolefully, his arms folded across his chest, his sturdy shoulder propped against the doorframe. Without giving him another look, she sat on the edge of the bed to remove her stockings and heels, depositing them in the sack.

"The big scene down there lost something in the translation," he eventually announced with an arrogant glint in his eye.

She popped up from the mattress, sparing him a harried look as she eased past toward the bathroom across the hall. "Oh, yeah?"

"Yeah." He shifted position slightly to watch her as she yanked open the medicine cabinet. "About three hundred sixty-nine dollars' worth."

She rolled her eyes, returning with a toothbrush and cosmetics. "Obviously, I spent the rest on expenses, Mr. Turner. The monied-executive-wife look doesn't come cheap." He grabbed her arm as she passed. With a startled cry, she instantly wrenched away. "Don't you dare start making husband noises about the budget!"

What had flashed through her eyes at the moment of contact? Fear? Panic? She'd definitely been singed by his touch. His mouth quirked with the provocative discovery. So he hadn't imagined her response to his kiss at the restaurant. It had been difficult to tell where the playacting began and ended. But there was an undeniable magnetic energy between them. And it had reached a level of urgency that was nearly choking him.

And she was about to walk out. He could sense the determination in her stride, the flat finality in her voice. And being temporarily barefoot and without a vehicle wouldn't stop her for long. Hiding her sneakers and refusing to drive her home certainly wouldn't keep her grounded. She was far too angry, far too innovative.

"If I handled things badly, Mad, I'm sorry," he conceded, apology the only weapon that came to mind. "Naturally, I was looking out for my own best interests with Swain. I just thought you were up to the challenge of handling this arrangement in clear-cut business terms."

"Oh, so did I!" Madeline agreed candidly. She tossed the toiletries into her sack and leaned against the dresser. "My revenge was spontaneous and heavily dosed with overkill. I probably shouldn't have taken on the job in the first place, considering how angry I've been over losing you as a client. I convinced myself that you were deliberately taking advantage of me tonight—"

"I wasn't!"

"You sold me down in the bar." She raised a halting palm. "Your surprise was obviously genuine. And I should've know better from the start. Men usually aren't that calculating, especially on such short notice.

I've come to realize that your looting of my perks was the impulsive act of a desperate man. You aren't accustomed to lying and pulled out every stop in sight. If nothing else, it should give you a new appreciation for my special Just Like a Wife touches."

"Appreciating you has never been in question," he assured her. "Just ask Eddie or Vic."

"No need," she said with forced nonchalance. "We'll just have to cut our losses. You can find yourself a new maid, and I'll find myself a new fifth husband."

She made a visual sweep of the bedroom, her chin beginning to wobble, her nose wrinkling in a sniff. Trey grimaced at the sight. After selling herself as the epitome of hip bravado, she was now playing the pouting, pitiful waif? It wasn't fair for her to give his heartstrings this unexpected tug. She'd spent the entire evening sizzling him to the crispy stage. To douse the fires with whipping cream seemed like a criminal maneuver.

"Say, Mad, you aren't by any chance blaming me for this sad end, are you?"

"Well, no Clancy has ever admitted to being wrong about anything," she said dubiously. "But I guess it's fair to say that it did take two to create this fiasco...."

A moment of electrical silence hung between them. Trey couldn't keep his eyes off her as she stood frozen in place, her hip wedged against his dresser. She reminded him of a caged kitten, without her heels, her hose. Oddly enough, it was the sweetest sight he'd ever seen. The strong, sassy lady teetering on the edge of vulnerability. Heaven help him, it only made her all the more sexy. She'd gotten under his skin, all right. In the form of a high-grade fever. Suddenly, the idea of letting her get away without a tumble and a taste caused something deep within his belly to clench.

He took a long look into her eyes and miraculously found the seeds of desire in their silvery depths. He'd seen that shimmer often enough to recognize it. But Mad's shell would be tougher than average to crack. She was born to bicker, to banter, to win. She'd have to show signs of a meltdown, some signal of encouragement.

As if catching his vibes, her hands jumped to her arms to rub away an involuntary shiver.

"I didn't mean to shake you up," he promptly lied, intent on calling attention to her condition.

"I am not shook!" she flared, lurching away from the dresser.

"Rattled? Frazzled?" he pressed.

"You're the one who's quaking in his socks!" she accused with a leveling finger.

"What red-blooded man wouldn't be?" he roared with levee-bursting force. "You swing those hips into overdrive and damn near hypnotize a man!"

She gaped at him. "I do?"

"Of course you do. And it doesn't seem to matter what you're wearing," he went on in despair. "Even in this conservative dress tonight, you . . . you—"

"Got you revved?" she finished with a measure of awe.

"Lord help me, yes!" He threw his hands up in disgust.

"Maybe I'd better be going," Madeline suggested in a wary voice. "We obviously both need a good night's rest—"

"I may never rest again!" he snapped. "I'm so wound up over you I can't see straight."

"So what are we going to do with you, Five?" To her own annoyance, her voice cracked slightly with the query. "Well?" she demanded in a stronger tone. Her stomach looped as he wordlessly zeroed in on her in predatory fashion. With his tie pulled loose on his snowy, unbuttoned collar, his dark gray suit jacket slightly open, his pants sharply creased, he could have stepped off a magazine cover. He was so like the prototype male she'd been searching for in the first place—tall, dark, virile, volatile.

Trapped together in her ex-husband's bedroom, mad at each other, madder *for* each other... The realization of their location and condition heightened with his every step, until Madeline was literally vibrating with sexual awareness. By the time they stood toe-to-toe, she was dizzy and weak with wanting. Sheer spunk alone rooted her to the spot.

"Brave enough to admit it, Mad?" he prodded, studying her keenly. "Confess that you feel it, too?"

Her sigh held surrender. "The attraction has been there. Right from the start."

His rigid jaw slackened. "Then why—?"

"Why didn't I invite you up to your place for a night-cap?" she finished breathlessly.

"Yes!"

Madeline wrung her hands as she sought the proper phrasing. The last thing she wanted him to do was laugh, or see her as some sort of suburban ninny. "I enjoy the flirt, the chase, the whole dating game. But I only play it out to the end with a man I know something about. Even my blind dates don't come with a completely blank slate," she confessed with effort. "I know many things about them in advance. You—you were a genuine stranger! It's never wise for a lady to take chances, so—"

"That's a more than reasonable reason!" he cut in with pleasure.

She blinked in surprise. He'd been expecting unreasonable? The man's face was actually sheeted with relief, of all things! It must have really damaged his ego, her not inviting him in. There was no other explanation. The idea that she could wound him on a personal level was a profound, heady discovery, and it made him all the more accessible, all the more devastating.

"I don't think we should dwell on what could have happened had I invited you up here the other night, or what would have happened if we'd discovered our link to one another," she asserted gently. "Either scenario may have done us in. I believe in fate, Trey. I believe things happen the way they are supposed to happen."

"I feel rather awkward with you, Mad," he faltered. "I feel you have the inside track on me and know just where my buttons are. I can't say I have the same advantage over you."

"Is there something you wish I didn't know?" she prodded softly.

"No, not exactly. I guess I just want to explain my feelings on marriage, on commitment.... Vic's argument that I don't test the waters wasn't expressed very well. I've come close to marrying a few times. Lived with a lady or two in my day, as well. I just don't have much insight when choosing a partner. Perhaps it's because I've always been so wrapped up in my work, or maybe it's because I just don't have the knack. Anyway, I've made some mistakes."

"As we all do, Trey," she hastened to assure him.

"Yeah, but recovery time for me takes a while. I'm intense during and after. The whole process makes me a rather a reluctant candidate for matrimony."

"You sound like a careful candidate to me," she argued with a bolstering smile.

"Vic tell you anything about Bonny?"

She blinked. "No. Was she the last one?"

"Yes. What a disastrous choice. All she did was eat gumdrops and watch television." He gazed at her in challenge. "So what do you think of that flub?"

"Well, that explains the rock-hard gumdrops I've been finding everywhere," she said.

"Oh, Madeline," he lamented, "one minute I feel you know too much about me, the next minute I feel you don't have a clue."

"I believe I've had a crash course today on the subject of you," she admitted softly. After hearing of his mother's string of relationships, Mad was certain that Trey had deliberately numbed himself from such intimate involvement, adopting a pay-your-way attitude to protect his feelings. From the moment they'd met, she'd been forcing him to dig deep for those buried emotions. And now she found herself confronted with the charged-up result. "And I definitely like what I see. A lot."

"Are you attracted to me?" he pressed, a husky note in his voice.

"Yes." She was lost for a more eloquent comeback, but it didn't seem to matter. That one breathless word brought a shudder to his body.

"Do you ever wear an apron?" he asked abruptly.

Her forehead creased. "No. Should I?"

"There are times when it would be nice...."

His eager, wolfish look startled her momentarily. Then she knew. It was a fantasy of some kind! So he had been thinking of her, perhaps quite a lot.... A thrill of ticklish anticipation coursed up her spine.

"Where are we going with this, Trey?"

"Heaven, I hope."

A pink tint crossed her cheeks as he visually measured her, roamed her body in seductive inventory. "I mean, our business arrangement as man and maid is over," she pointed out. "As is the free-lance job with Swain." She fingered his lapels, her eyes full of an uncertain yearning. "I feel that if we go on from here, it has to be on a new, fresh path with promise. Can you understand that?"

Trey understood. They'd reached either a crossroads or a dead end. And dead ends didn't deserve a tumble between the sheets—not with a classy, complex girl like Mad. Yes, she was obstinate, difficult and unrelenting in viewpoint. But oh, the power she put behind her chosen causes! His body threatened to shatter as he imagined Mad's capacity to love, to please, to seduce. And he'd never been so sure a woman wanted him. She was as blatantly open about her sexual wants as she was about everything else. There wasn't a hint of the teasing twinkle that normally danced in her eyes. Lust lingered there, a spark waiting to flare with one scrape of a match.

But she would walk out of his life without some encouragement, some sincerity, for she was a diva of discriminating tastes. An old-fashioned Tuckahoe girl at heart.

Trey cupped her face in his hands, brushing his thumbs over her jawline. "It could be only the beginning for us, in so many ways, Mad," he uttered thickly. "To my own amazement, the thought of letting you slip through my fingers before discovering all your secrets grows more impossible by the second." Those fingers began to move in exploration, pushing tides of her apricot hair away from her temples, touching her features with a measure of wonder.

"Hope you have a million years to spare," she whispered in warning, tipping her head back with a soft moan as his hands stroked the tender curve of her throat. "Because I have a million secrets."

"I know...." His touch continued downward, one hand bracing her back, the other undoing the front of her dress. She trembled in pleasure as his knuckles deliberately grazed her body with every button pop. One final brush sent the frock to the floor, leaving Madeline standing before him in a white satin slip.

Like a thirsty man dipping his face into a stream, Trey seized her shoulders and captured her mouth with his own, kissing her hotly, deeply, with a fierce yearning to taste and consume. Unlike the first time in the restaurant, he was certain she wouldn't pull away. And thanks to the first time, he knew what he was getting— the most succulent kiss a man could imagine.

And it proved to be only the beginning. With the sort of initiative he'd come to expect from Madeline, she made some bold moves herself. In a flash, her arms curled up round his neck and her tongue curled in round his teeth. Holding tightly to his solid frame, she pressed wantonly into him. Suddenly she was stunningly alive with aphrodisia, a satin-covered flame, hot and slippery beneath his eager hands, her tides of golden hair blinding his vision. She was drawing him into a frenzy with her, and he was still dressed in his suit.

He tore his mouth from hers with a gasp. "Hold on . . ." With swift movements, he began to tear at his clothes. It was no surprise to her that his fingers immediately fell to his belt. As he worked at his pants, she tangled with his tie, stripping it from his collar, breaking away to whirl it through the air like a lasso. Stepping out of his slacks and briefs, he made a grab for the loose end of the tie, yanking her back against him.

"Seems my slip and your shirt are the only things left between us," she purred.

"And presumably your panties," he rasped.

"Better check your facts," she invited, her hands cupping his buttocks beneath his shirttail, pressing his groin between her thighs.

With an impatient growl, Trey reached for the hem of her slip and pulled it up to her head. There was nothing covering her satin cream hips, the hair-dusted juncture at her thighs. He stood admiring her sculptured form for a long delicious moment.

"Get this thing off of me!" Her cry was muffled by the garment bunched up over her face.

Trey tugged off the slip and tossed it aside. "You went out tonight without panties?" he demanded in disbelief. "Played my demure little woman without panties?"

"Yeah, I did," she flared, standing naked and defiant before him.

He gaped at her with a measure of appreciation and awe. "But why?"

"Because I felt so confined in that plain, ordinary dress. I needed to feel foxy underneath it all. Just a little, to keep my spirits up."

Thank God he hadn't known about the exposed goddess at his side the entire evening. He would've been a blithering idiot at dinner, the horny kind of cad a traditional man like Swain would've just as soon dumped in the Hudson River! Trey's eyes blazed as he stripped away his shirt. This porcelain Venus wanted him! Never had a woman caused him so much distress, so much trouble—deliberately. He couldn't wait to burrow deep inside her. With a swift scoop she was in his arms. They landed side by side on the bed with a bounce, breathing hungrily, passionately.

"You're a confusion, honey," he lamented hoarsely. "But as Vic says, you're exciting...."

"Hah!" Madeline crawled over his sprawled form. "That's what he says about you, too!"

Trey's growl was lost on her lips as he guided her head down for another heady kiss. The outline of her body atop his was like a searing brand on his skin. His hands slipped down her back, pressing her silky length against his hair-roughened torso. His fingers glided up and over the curve of her hips, gently kneading her muscled bottom, bearing down to meld her pelvis into his erection. He groaned aloud as her nest of curls caused a glorious friction against his shaft. Madeline's fingers invaded the area like ten separate flames, bringing the burn to an exquisite, unbearable brink.

He seemed to be on the verge of explosion. But the tremors eddied and he was tipping her off. With a panther roll, he straddled her smooth, flat stomach. Cupping the underside of one breast, then the other, he dipped down to nuzzle her nipples to life. She cradled his head, lavishing in the sensations of his moist suckling. She arched beneath him as the pull on her turgid buds reached clear down to her most feminine place.

Trey could feel her arched body responding, her thighs squeezing his rib cage in a timeless signal. Placing a hand beneath her curved spine, he slid down her torso with fluid grace, licking a trail of wet fire to her navel. Landing at the foot of the mattress, he gently pushed her up against the bank of pillows at the headboard. Her knees instinctively fell open and he parted them further, tasting, caressing the inside of her satin thighs until she cried out in wonder.

With a supple movement, he reached into the nightstand for protection. Swiftly sheathing himself, he entered her with a single deep thrust. With a look of sheer bedevilment, Mad suddenly locked him inside with a muscle clench, causing him to cry out in wonder. It was an unexpected reminder that with her, the surprises never ended. At the same heart-stopping moment, Trey felt lost in her and found in paradise.

Time oozed slowly ahead on their liquid, honeyed journey. Madeline was delighted to find that Trey brought his rigid control from the boardroom to the bedroom, without his trademark impatience and demand for quick results. Indeed, he was the master of forbearance as he drove himself to the brink numerous times, and her to a solo capitulation once, before mounting her for a mutual flight.

They rocked together to a shattering pinnacle, alert enough to whisper encouragement and endearments.

She exploded around him first, digging her fingernails into his taut shoulder muscles. Tremors rocketed through his body soon after. Slick with sweat, satisfied and exhausted, they collapsed in the damp, tangled sheets.

Madeline wasn't sure how long they'd been dozing when she sat up in bed with a start. Thankfully, the room was still black, a comforting signal that darkness still cloaked the city. She whisked the sheet away and climbed over Trey's snoozing form toward the nightstand. The clock radio read 3:10.

"C'mon, Five, time to roll!" With a smack on his bare hip, she slipped off the bed.

Rising up on his elbows, he regarded sleepily. "What's the matter, Mad?"

She was already easing back into her dress. "I have to go home."

"Now?"

"Yes!"

Trey's irritation roused him swiftly. He bolted up, his heavy brows narrowed. "Don't tell me that at twenty-five you still have a curfew. Or are you sneaking back before the neighbors see?"

To his amazement, she laughed. "I live at home for a lot of reasons. But the need for supervision is not one of them! As for the neighbors, their comments would only be fodder to the controversy-hungry Clancys. We'll take an opposing stand on almost anything, just for the thrill of the debate. Besides, everybody in the neighborhood is trying to fix me up. They all know somebody in the city, and they all know about your apartment."

Her manhunt setup still rankled him, but he forced himself to focus on this new frustration. "Then why do you have to go?"

She sat down beside him, shoving her bare feet into sneakers. "Because I have four husbands to take care of."

He'd forgotten. During their short erotic interlude, he'd left all the baggage behind. Now it was slapping him in the face, while the night was still romantic velvet. "This doesn't seem right," he protested. "I'm the man who's staked a claim, spoken of tomorrows, and I don't count anymore. I'm not even your fifth anymore."

She reached over to cup his face in her hands. "Now, darling, try to be sensible. You know you can never be Five again. Our intimacy has made that impossible. I am strictly a platonic wife for hire."

"I should hope so!" he roared, wrenching out of reach. He prowled the room in naked splendor, envisioning her in that sheer apron again. But it was torment this time to see her that way, while they were talking of the other husbands she so diligently nurtured.

"It's just a job," she reiterated. "I make a living keeping a happy home for single men. I'm not emotionally involved in their lives. It's all part of the image, the package. Why, I'd burn out in a month if I allowed these guys to draw me into all of their trials and tribulations. There is absolutely nothing to be jealous of."

"I am not jealous! I just feel cheated."

"Well, you shouldn't," she shot back tersely, shifting on the edge of the mattress. "I've given you the most I can give any man."

"I know you've given me that," he hastened to admit on a softer note. "And it was wonderful. Can't you see it makes this dead-of-night exit all the tougher to take?"

"I can't help it," she returned hotly. "All I see is your selfishness. Your unreasonableness. You knew all about my job before we did the mattress tango."

"I know! There was just no way I could resist. I simply find myself reacting to you, with no forethought or reasoning involved at all," he lamented, perplexed.

"You make me sound like a mind-altering drug!"

She flung her head back to confront his towering figure, causing her lush apricot hair to tumble over her shoulders. Trey blinked at her fiery features and flashing eyes, finding it impossible to disclaim the accusation.

"Do you have any tangible feelings at all for me?" she demanded with a mixture of desperation and irritation. "Anything that reaches your mind?"

Trey nodded with a deep sigh. "Yes! Of course. I'm just having a bit of trouble accepting that I'm helpless in your hands. I like to control when and how I feel. You've stolen that away from me."

Madeline flinched slightly under his accusatory look. "I'm sorry I've forced you into such a tizzy."

"The crime is to dump me right after we made love," he muttered. "This is a time when we should be together—talking, cuddling."

They'd been sleeping, but she decided not to quibble. "I didn't know this was going to happen tonight," she reasoned. "I always intended to be home way before sunrise. You as well as anyone know how demanding a business can be. I have obligations to meet tomorrow. I can't make an exception this time, right before Thanksgiving."

Trey rubbed his face with his hands as he wrestled with her logic. How many times had he crawled out of some lady's bed to catch a plane, meet a client? "It wouldn't be so bad if you had a different sort of job," he attempted to argue.

"Maybe, maybe not," she returned, easing off the bed. "At any rate, I have to leave. Are you still planning to drive me home?"

"Yes," he told her retreating figure. "Madeline," he called out after several beats.

She paused by the door, slowly turning in hope. "Yes?"

His gaze wavered indecisively, as though searching his soul for the proper response. Even in all his creativity, however, he couldn't manage to express himself. "Just—just give me a minute to pull myself together."

8

TREY COULDN'T HELP but stifle yawn after yawn the next morning as he and Vic waited for Swain at Creative Works headquarters. They were seated in Trey's private office, at a desk littered with slogans and drawings concerning the Swain baby-food account. Trey felt like crawling atop the heap of paper for a long, dreamless nap. As it was, he couldn't resist spreading his forearms on the desk top and hunching over it. Vic found himself constantly shoving Trey's arms one way, then the other, as he organized the sketches.

"Are you moaning and mumbling because you want to talk about her?" the artist finally asked in exasperation.

Trey swiveled in his chair to confront his friend, noting for the first time that Vic had taken pains to shed his hippie image for the meeting. He hadn't popped for a suit, but he had opted for a tan corduroy sports jacket and cotton slacks. His salt-and-pepper mane had been pruned to a nice shape and his face had a shaven, apple-cheeked look.

"Let's stick to business."

"Well, you're in the deep stuff either way," Vic predicted. "What's this old guy got on his mind, anyhow, fancying himself on the label of his own baby-food line?"

"Immortality," Trey responded in a defensive tone.

"I have the feeling you hired me on here not for my creative input, but because I do one hell of a portrait. Now, isn't that the awful truth?"

"I don't want to argue with you, Vic," Trey said in way of affirmation.

"Swain is just too . . . too dapper, too David Niven-ish to be pushing pabulum," Vic insisted.

"I have to make it work. Perhaps have a small sketch of him in the center of some clever, camouflaging layout. We could do it, if artistic egos were left at the door."

Vic released a long whistle between his teeth. "Okay, okay. Walking out on you now would be like leaving a wounded deer in a ditch."

Trey's jawline hardened and his eyes glimmered with new energy. "The hell it would! I'm fine, dammit!"

"Look, I know she spent some after-hours time in your place last night—"

"Nosy neighbor."

"Talk to me, old buddy! You'll never convince Swain all is well in the newlywed nest if you don't clear your mind."

Trey ran his fingers through his already tousled hair. "I hoped to get a handle on Mad with a little digging, but I'm more confused than ever now," he lamented, pitching a pencil across the room. "Could there be such a thing as the perfect woman? I mean, a glorious package with all the options—support, seduction, beauty, brains?"

"You've got the whipped-pup syndrome," Vic diagnosed without hesitation, rubbing a hand over his growing grin. "Lay back and accept it."

"You don't understand!" Trey objected vehemently. "I'm asking for your objective opinion on the issue of a dream wife. Mad seems to be capable of any task. So cool, so hot, so capable.... You should've seen her torturing me right under Swain's nose last night. It was downright diabolical."

"You liked being tortured?"

"Of course not," he scoffed impatiently. "The point is that she did it so charmingly. All men seem utterly mad for her. Even you."

"Guilty," Vic admitted with a nod. He leaned back in his chair, lacing his fingers over his fleshy midriff.

"Surviving four marriages should make you something of an expert," Trey pressed. "Ever run into a wife with everything?"

"I'd be short at least one divorce if I had," Vic assured him. "You're going overboard with this dissection. Marriage is a personal deal, choosing the proper mate a subjective affair!"

"Who said anything about getting married?" Trey thundered, nearly bouncing backward in his spring-loaded chair.

"Wake up, Trey!" Vic chastised with a laugh. "You're upset because you've stumbled across the right woman for you. The only woman for you. It shoots your perennial-bachelor plans right down the tubes. I'm an expert at spotting that smitten, glazed-over look in a man—seen it in my own mirror often enough. Face it. Deal with it. The only thing you've got to lose is your stake in the singles manual you and Eddie are putting together." A silence fell between them, causing Vic to study him in suspicious scrutiny. "So, just how did you blow this setup?"

"I didn't!"

"When are you going to see her again, then?"

"I don't know for certain. . . ."

Vic jabbed an accusing finger at him. "You let her get away!"

Trey adjusted the lapels of his charcoal-colored suit. "Only as far as Tuckahoe."

"Might as well be the moon, considering its suburban diversity," Vic objected anxiously. "Let's see here... First you fired her, then, rather than trusting her enough to rehire her, you took her on free-lance. Then you made love to her. Then you shuffled her back to Tuckahoe—without a word about tomorrow, right?"

"I began with the best intentions. The best. But I ended up a little steamed," Trey begrudgingly admitted. "She, uh, couldn't even stay the night, for crissake! Had to get back to her four husbands." The last words twisted sourly across his tongue.

"How long do you think you'll have to absorb the shock of your own self-discoveries?" Vic asked in challenge. "Matrimony fits Mad like a hand in a glove. You should be that glove, man, wrapping her up forever. This is your chance for a fulfilling life. You've got a nubile beauty on the string who's searching for a successful prince. Only the dumbest toad in the pond would croak on objectively about it."

"I'm gun-shy about commitment," he blurted out in despair. "Dammit, she even figured out why—because of my mother's dismal failures!" He closed his eyes, envisioning their ardent lovemaking. Such fire, such sweetness. And knowing all the while that this sexy siren could run a household like Hazel. . . . Remarkable.

Three short warning buzzes from Sue Parker at reception alerted them to Swain's arrival. The tycoon entered moments later, his cheery, distinguished self.

Trey wasn't certain if it was relevant, but there seemed to be an odd sparkle in Swain's eye. Trey was well schooled in reading both current clients and potential ones. His instincts told him that Swain wasn't going to sign on and sign off in one simple swoop. There was no cab downstairs with the meter running.

"Good morning, fellows," he greeted smoothly, shaking the hand Vic offered him.

Trey made a swift introduction and then settled Swain into a comfortable leather chair opposite him at the desk. Then he began to shuffle through papers, showing Swain some of the concepts that had been embellished upon since their last meeting in Los Angeles. Swain poured over them carefully, puffing his pipe to life after asking politely if either men objected. Trey and Vic exchanged a hopeful look as Swain smoked and pondered. As his gaze strayed more and more frequently toward the door, Trey felt compelled to ask him if there was something he needed.

"I was wondering if Madeline would be joining you for lunch today," he intoned with urbane charm.

"Sorry, no," Trey swiftly replied, busily rearranging the angle of his telephone.

Swain's six-foot frame seemed to deflate in the chair. "Such a shame. Perhaps if you called the apartment . . ."

The last place she'd be, Trey thought dourly. "She's with her mother today," he improvised, forcing cheer into his voice under Vic's warning glance.

"Joanna's in the city!" Swain rejoiced in assumption. "A double treat, surely."

The cause of the twinkle was getting clearer. Swain had hoped to enjoy Madeline's company again today.

Drat and damnation. Trey opened his desk drawer in search of a pen. "I'm afraid that the ladies are in Tuckahoe, Swain. But if you'd like to sign this contract, I'm sure we can find the perfect spot for a celebration lunch."

Swain ignored the pen poised in the air between them. "Will she be back this afternoon?"

Trey flashed him a regretful smile as he formulated a feasible story. "Madeline won't be back at all until after Thanksgiving. You see, we intend to have our turkey with Joanna and the family. I'll, uh, be joining them Wednesday evening."

"How marvelous! How delightful! Big family gatherings are so full of goodwill."

Trey didn't know firsthand, but he nodded in agreement. The blood was slowly draining from the hand holding the pen, but he held it steady with the highest of hopes.

"I've had a disappointing turn this morning," Swain confided, leaning away from the desk to puff on his pipe. "My daughter Jennifer had invited me to join her family in Ohio for Thanksgiving dinner, but the kids have come down with the measles, and it would be too risky for me to be around them." Swain's eyes centered on Trey in blunt anticipation. He wanted to join the brood in Tuckahoe.

Trey understood why such an invitation would seem like a simple request to Swain. How could one more guest be an intrusion? In fact, it couldn't be a bigger imposition, with Trey having no wife, no family, no turkey, even, to call his own.

"I plan to stay here in the city through the holiday now," Swain went on, taking another tack. "It'll give me ample time to go over these campaigns, make a final decision about Creative Works. Can you recommend a restaurant, one that's putting on an old-fashioned family feast?"

"You shouldn't be alone, dwelling on business," Trey objected with good grace, accepting that Swain had him over a barrel. "If you'd like, I could consult Madeline about setting another place at our table for you." He nearly broke the unused pen in half as he withdrew his hand.

"Oh, really?" Swain examined his pipe as though weighing the novel idea. "I wouldn't want to impose."

Oh really, my ass, Trey thought. The guy was a silk-covered steamroller! As Mad was a petulant satin doll. How had he allowed himself to become sandwiched between them this way? He gritted his teeth over the impending price tag. Financially and emotionally, the figure was bound to be a whopper.

"CALL FOR YOU on the wife line, Madness!" Peter's message, echoing hollowly up the basement stairwell, instantly drew Madeline's attention. Still gripping the silver candlestick she'd been polishing at the kitchen table, she raced across the room, a pink streak in her comfortable old sweats. She came to a sharp halt at the doorway, glaring down at the twelve-year-old. "I didn't know you were in the office. You'd better not be playing games on my computer. It's been so touchy lately and we can't afford to have the repairman back."

The young genius reared back in insult, a sheaf of white-blond hair falling into his eyes. "Such things are for children like Benj. I'm far too busy for such nonsense."

"Look, if it's another prospective Five on the phone, I don't have the time to speak to him until Saturday." Joanna and Granny Dot had already taken it upon themselves to post flyers around the local shops advertising for a Friday husband. "As a matter of fact, that's what I want you to tell all of them from now on."

"It's your ex-Five," Peter reported with a trace of irritation. "For a couple of bucks I would tell him where to fly—"

"Don't you dare!" she screeched frantically.

Peter shrugged in bewilderment. "What are you so sore about? You've got four husbands eager to pay for your attention. This guy is history. You said so yourself."

"Professionally he's history. But personally he's extremely current."

Peter's freckled face wrinkled. "Oh, jeez. You've got an errand list a mile long for the lucrative ones, and you're juiced up over Turner."

"You are far too focused on profit margins," Madeline scolded.

"If you were stuck wearing your grandma's glasses out in public, you'd be looking for some fast money, too!"

Madeline felt a momentary stab of remorse as she headed for the phone on the kitchen counter. She'd been planning to give her brother last night's leftover thirty-one dollars. But Peter's dilemma had been forgotten in her foolish fit of righteous indignation. It was only after she'd given the cash back to Trey and was marching toward the elevator that she remembered who she'd been saving it for. Peter would just have to be patient. Nearly every nickel was accounted for these days. It would take some creative corner-cutting to fill the poor kid's mayonnaise jar with the required one hundred and thirty dollars.

With a steadying sigh, she set down the candlestick and punched the blinking button on the telephone. Maybe Trey was calling to apologize. Frankly, she'd be grateful if he was simply willing to talk things over. The silence in the car last night on the journey back to Tuckahoe had been excruciating. Clancys never let things get bottled up inside that way. But she had easily sensed that Trey was in no condition to discuss his feelings. He was too intent on blaming her for them! And she saw little difference between his feeling jealous and his feeling cheated over her necessary departure. He was envious of the time and attention she bestowed on her husbands. But it was her job, for heaven's sake! As if she was attracted to any of those guys.

"Hello, Trey?" she lilted, her pulse leaping in anticipation.

"I'm in big trouble and it's all your fault!"

Madeline held the receiver a few inches from her ear as Trey poured out his tale of Swain and the frozen-food king's plans to stay here because of a measles epidemic in Ohio. His refusal to sign on the dotted line. His interest in the Tuckahoe turkey feast.

"Simmer down," she said at last.

"What were you thinking of, describing your mother as a cross between Loni Anderson and Marilyn Monroe? Your brothers as the precocious Wally and Beaver Cleaver boys? Not to mention the stern but fair Granny Dot, Tuckahoe's answer to Ann Landers."

"Surely you don't think I deliberately bragged about my family just to lure Swain here for Thanksgiving! The last thing I need is another man to wine and dine this week!"

"Well, you were troweling it on heavily, knowing that he was a sucker for family life," he tossed back. "Knowing that I had no family of my own to embellish on."

"I talk about them naturally, Trey," she hastily assured him. "It was harmless conversation on my part. Let's face it, my stories filled what could have been awkward lapses of silence."

"Yes, but at the same time, it intrigued him beyond normal proportions. Now he's anxious for more."

"I didn't do it deliberately," she maintained firmly. "You hired me to help guide his pen to the dotted line, and I acted with the best intentions."

Trey made a doubtful noise. "I'd be willing to believe you might regret what you did after we, uh, did what we did...."

"I didn't bait Swain! And if you don't believe me, that's tough. I have troubles of my own. One had some kind of pizza spill in his oven, so I have to remedy that before we can pop in his turkey Thursday morning. Two's luggage was lost on a trip to Japan, so I have to go buy him a half-dozen shirts and ties before he sets off for Germany. Three misplaced his mother's antique candlesticks, so I had to tear his attic apart in search of them." She surveyed the half-polished object on the counter. "They are currently covered in tarnish, and it'll take me forever to bring them back to their original luster." Madeline knew she sounded like a huffy

housewife on a TV commercial, but she lived like one.
Trey might as well come to understand it.

"I guess a guy really does have to take a number to
be noticed by you."

"He sure does today!" she heartily agreed.

"You know what your problem is? You're just too
damn good to be true."

"Just what do you mean?"

"Don't play the innocent. You create the ideal nest for
the average bachelor, then make it impossible for him
to live without you. Your apron strings stretch for miles
in all directions."

"You've really got a thing for aprons."

"A *Mad* thing."

As hard as she fought, Madeline couldn't stop images of their intimacy from flooding her senses. She
closed her eyes for a shaky moment, feeling a surge of
pleasure, followed by an eddy of loss. He'd contacted
her to complain, not to reconcile their differences.

"Look, if you called to chew me out for being too nice
to Swain, for being too good to be true, consider the job
done." With a disgusted *humph*, she hung up. Seconds
later, the phone rang again. "Hello," she purred. "Just
Like a Wife."

"I didn't call to complain. I called to ask you for the
obvious favor."

"Oh, sure. Quick, catch me while I'm still all but-
tered up," she invited sarcastically.

"You owe me, Mad," he asserted offensively. "Don't
you understand you've toppled my personal empire and
are about to do the same to my professional one? I had
the perfect setup for the easy-livin' bachelor business-

man. A host of hot chicks from Manhattān to L.A. A social calendar organized to the letter. Clean socks. Fresh sheets. Your expert backup prepared me to face the world day and night. Why'd you have to go and niggle underneath my skin and spoil it all?"

"Did I ever pick the wrong bed to dive into!" she exclaimed in disgust. "Whether you're in it with me or not, it's nothing but a losing proposition!"

The masculine groan on the line was weighted with pain and frustration. "I haven't had a lucid thought since we parted," he confessed unhappily. "You're right about the apron strings. I'm bound like a mummy and cursed like one, too. Unless you bail me out, that is."

Madeline squeezed the receiver, tempted to hang up again. One last dial tone would serve him right. He'd known exactly what he was getting into when he'd made love to her. And he knew she expected more than a one-nighter. If only he could acknowledge his emotions, admit that they were ruling his behavior. It wasn't a crime to be jealous of her platonic husbands, but it was criminal not to admit the frailty to himself. He was literally killing their budding relationship with his pouting over the demands of her profession. It was just a job to her! A job which, with a little understanding on his part, could be totally separate from their personal liaison. The fact that he continually used money as a lever to get his way only made hiding from his heart all the easier. And he was about to do it again—draw upon her time and skills in the form of another freelance job.

Trey cleared his throat on the silent line. "Mad, I'm in a hell of a jam. Swain refuses to sign. He's openly blackmailing me into getting him this Thanksgiving invitation. You've got him dreaming of everything from your bread stuffing to your mother's curvaceous charms. The stuffing I could buy here in the city— throw it together with a frozen turkey breast and some limp lie. But the family ambience is another matter entirely. And I'm out of your house wine," he added as an afterthought. "I have a half-dozen different bottles stacked up here on my desk and none of them even come close to yours."

"So you have been entertaining the thought of entertaining him yourself," she surmised in annoyance.

"Well, you're mad if I do and mad if I don't!" he shot back. "Are you going to help me out or not?"

"I'll do it," she agreed. "We'll have a Clancy conference and I'll get back to you with the details."

His relief was audible. "Thank you so much. I'm afraid I already told him I'm expected Wednesday night. But, naturally, I expect to pay for all the inconveniences this will cause," he hastily assured her.

"Oh, no you don't!" She inveighed under her breath for his ears only. "You're not weaseling out of this with your wallet. This is a bona fide favor. On the house from start to finish."

"Nothing in this world is free," he argued suspiciously.

"There is one obvious condition, of course. I expect you to think about us in a calmer, more reasonable manner. If you don't want to focus on a future, I never want to hear from you again after the holiday. Understood?"

"Makes sense to me."

"Well, you don't have to sound so damn surprised that it does!" This time she did hang up. With a bang!

"Who has you in such a tizzy?" Granny Dot demanded, emerging from the basement with a laundry basket full of clean clothes.

Gripping her candlestick, Madeline returned to the table. "Five."

Granny Dot set the basket on the opposite side of the table with a thump. "Causes more havoc now than he did while you were on his payroll!"

Joanna entered from the hallway just in time to hear Dot's remark. "Who, Five?"

"Yes, Mom," Madeline replied with strained patience as she dipped her small rag into the jar of silver polish. "It seems my role as Five's fake real wife isn't over yet."

"Really?" Peter asked, shooting through the basement doorway with Benji on his heels. "He have another free-lance job in mind?" Peter's eyes twinkled greedily as he ogled his sister for answers.

"It seems Swain refuses to sign on with Five until after he has Thanksgiving here." To Madeline's relief, all four faces expressed intense interest in the new angle.

"How very odd," Granny Dot clucked, adjusting the laundry basket so Joanna could join in on the sock-sorting task.

"I'm afraid Five is a little annoyed with me for making all of you sound just too wonderful," she explained matter-of-factly as she polished.

"Five has nothing to fear," Joanna cooed, matching a black sock with a blue one. "We'll help him out. Why, entertaining Harvey Swain will be a pleasure. He sounds just so dishy!"

Granny Dot snatched the odd socks from her daughter-in-law's hands with a *humph*. "Your head is already in the clouds and we haven't even begun to prepare things."

"They want to come Wednesday night," Madeline reluctantly reported. She was met with the expected series of groans. "We'll have to work out sleeping arrangements."

"Indeed we will," Granny Dot bellowed, squinting from behind her wire rims. "This Swain fellow believes you're married to Five. How can we explain the fact that he isn't sleeping in your room?"

"Leave it to me and Benj," Peter inserted with authority. "We'll come up with something plausible, won't we, Benj?"

"Sure will," Benji squeaked, openly anxious to be part of the plan.

"Having Five retire after Swain does seem like the easiest way," Joanna proposed. "Once the older man is closed away in our guest room, Five can move right in with the boys. Sleep in the top bunk above Peter. We'll rouse him early and Swain will never know. We can handle that for two nights, I'm sure."

Granny Dot nodded her gray head. "Yes, I imagine they'll want to stay over until Friday morning. We'll have to formulate some common facts for chitchat. Such as how long you've been married to Five. Where you were married—things like that."

"Married in Vegas, honeymooned in Tahoe," Madeline reported thoughtfully. "And I have a pager because you folks like to keep in touch with me."

This news brought on a round of laughter.

"Five didn't make any remarks about us, did he?" Granny Dot wondered suddenly. "You know what I mean—like claiming that we traveled together somewhere or that we make his favorite goulash?"

"Fortunately, he only went out on one limb," Madeline haltingly confessed. "And when he did it, he certainly didn't think Swain would ever be meeting her."

Joanna blinked as her daughter's pitying gaze swung toward her. "What did he say?"

"He mentioned to Swain that you and he enjoy a good game of canasta on occasion."

"Imagine," Granny Dot crowed in delight. "Our Joanna sitting still for a game of cards!"

"What a crummy liar!" Joanna flared indignantly. "A man his age should know how to tell a simple fib, shouldn't he? False remarks—especially to strangers—should take in a broader scope. The proper lie would've been something about the whole Clancy family liking cards."

"Lying is a talent some never master," Madeline retorted in defense. "He was in a panic because I was lathering on the praise. He desperately wanted to appear to belong to us. So you see, it's really my fault."

Granny Dot frowned. "A Clancy volunteering to take the blame? You aren't falling for this Five character, are you?"

"Of course she's in love with him!" Joanna announced wistfully, waving a knee-high sock. "Aren't you, Maddy dear? Why, it's written all over you."

"Why else would she have been out well past the twelve o'clock deadline last night?" Peter hooted in agreement. "If he'd paid her overtime, she'd have told us."

"My love life isn't the issue right now!" Madeline insisted. She wasn't prepared to reveal her innermost feelings for Trey yet, to watch her intuitive clan dissect the intimacy out of this most promising relationship.

"Nosiree, we've got a hot job to do," Peter concurred joyously. "This free-lance work from Five is really stacking up. The profits must be enormous."

All eyes centered on Madeline. How could she tell them there would be not a nickel from last night or the scam to come? She couldn't. They wouldn't put their hearts into their in-law parts if they knew it was charity, a lesson to a disillusioned man leaning on a crutch of cash. And this was something she had to do for Trey. If she could prove there was such a thing as unconditional love, selfless motivation, he just might open up and commit to her.

"There will be plenty of time to count up the booty," Madeline assured them, with a dismissive wave of her polishing rag. "I'm sure all of you have rooms to clean and chores to do. I'm going to call Five back to confirm, then devote the rest of the afternoon to my other husbands. Can't afford to let them down, either."

"No, indeed," the ever-practical Granny Dot agreed.

"But how am I to learn canasta by tomorrow night?" Joanna fretted.

All eyes fell on their resident genius. "What's in it for me?" he demanded petulantly. "I'll have to go to the library for a book on cards, teach myself the game, then turn around and teach Mom. And Benji will want to play, too. He always does."

"This family sticks together," Joanna proclaimed with a toss of her auburn head. "We're a team."

"Oh, all right," he grumbled.

"Okay then, Clancys," Madeline proclaimed, jumping to her feet. "We have the game plan. One, two, three—break!"

9

IT WAS AROUND EIGHT o'clock the next night when Trey pulled his sleek black Jaguar up to the curb in front of the Clancy's Tuckahoe home. Their large Tudorstyle house sat well back in a spacious, tree-scattered yard, a single light burning at the stoop in welcome. Harvey Swain wasted no time unfolding his long frame from the low-slung car. Pausing on the boulevard to stretch his cramped limbs, he studied the moonlit property.

"Nice place," he remarked to Trey as the adman rounded the car with their modest-size suitcases.

"Yes." Trey anxiously ushered him up the curving walk. He wanted to get inside the house before Swain asked him any awkward question he couldn't answer, such as how old the Tudor was or how many bedrooms it had. Mad had promised that they'd guide him through the blind spots, fill in the blanks about their personal lives. They couldn't afford another bogus "fact" like the canasta one. He was to pull back and let them take the lead. It was frightful to put all his faith and trust in others. Especially without handing over a cent!

All he'd asked of the Clancys in return was that they not call him Five. His name was Trey, or James—or Turner, if they liked! But Swain would surely wonder about such a strange tag, and it would be a painful reminder to Trey that at best he was garnering only a fifth of Mad's attention. And now that he'd bowed out of his husbandly slot, he'd most likely end up with a sixth of her time! The notion wrenched his gut in ways it had never been wrenched before!

This territorial sensation was making his head swim too. Vic's assertion that Trey wanted Mad for himself was seeping slowly into his psyche. But what red-blooded male could resist the lure? Madeline Clancy was perfect wife material. It was enough to make this confirmed bachelor not so sure of his course any-more....

Trey took the four concrete steps in two strides and rang the bell. The door promptly swung open and there stood Mad. She was an absolute dream in green leggings and an oversize mint-colored sweater.

"Darling!" She stepped over the threshold to embrace him, her tide of apricot hair taking on a golden halo under the porch light.

The moment his hands touched her rib cage, he knew he couldn't resist kissing her. Her lips were painted a rich coral color, and when they parted in moist invitation, he swiftly dipped his head to consume them.

For most men in his position, it would have been a lark to pretend for a moment that this was his doorstep and Mad was his real wife, welcoming him home. But, as with this entire husbandly pretense, the kiss was a serious stretch for Trey. He was nearly trembling as she cooperatively looped her arms around his neck, drawing him lower for easy access. To his relief, she played it just right. Her fingers rested lightly on the collar of his leather jacket, and her body, while close, didn't undulate teasingly into his, leaving him too bothered to be seen in public.

They'd been locking lips for only a matter of seconds, but it seemed like an eternity to Trey. As he hungrily tasted and probed the sweet depths of her mouth, he was forced to admit that Mad did indeed have some inexplicable power over him. Was this what real love did to a man—leave him a churning force field of emotions about to explode in all directions? Dropping her off last night had seemed like an urgent mission at the time. The only way he'd seen to relieve the pressure building between them had been to flee the hopeless situation in which she served several men all too well.

But abstinence hadn't been the answer, either. With or without her, Trey felt doomed, a slave to his desire to completely monopolize her every thought, her every act.

He closed his eyes to prolong the blissful feeling, but found he couldn't suppress the raw fear suddenly eddying along the edges of his consciousness. This was just the sort of romantic fog in which his own mother frequently lost herself, in which Vic wandered on his way to the altar. Two of the people he loved most in the world kept coming to the marital feast, only to depart again, empty and alone.

Madeline obviously felt him stiffen, for she subtly released him. When Trey opened his eyes, he fully expected to find hers full of disgust, anger, disappointment. But all he found within their gray depths was comfort, an invitation to trust. She was a woman of endless surprises.

"Let's really put on the dog and entertain inside the house!" Granny Dot proposed abruptly over Madeline's shoulder. With a sharp yank, she drew her out of the way. "Good evening, Mr. Swain," she greeted in a honeyed voice, giving her pin-curled blue-gray cap a pat.

Madeline turned to find the Clancys lined up in the entryway like household staff on hand to meet the new estate owner. Scrubbed faces, bright eyes, pressed clothing…they would be ready to kill when they found out there was no financial profit to be gained!

"Please, call me Swain," the tall, distinguished man urged the group with a twinkle in his eye. The twinkle brightened to a dazzle as his gaze skimmed over Dot and the boys to alight on Joanna, posed coquettishly at the bottom of the open staircase. Madeline noted that her mother was dressed in black leggings similar to her own, but instead of a baggy sweater, she was wearing a form-fitting top of gold lamé.

"Delighted, Swain." The name rolled off Joanna's tongue like a musical note.

The executive strode across the tiled floor, his arms extended. Surveying his tweed jacket, crest of white hair and thin, aristocratic features, Madeline was again reminded of old-world chivalry, the kind so often featured in the romance novels Joanna absorbed by the dozen. *A child bride, a widow yet to bloom.*

"Care for a cup of coffee?" Joanna offered breathlessly.

"I'd love a cup of coffee," he intoned, his hand on her shoulder as they glided off together like a pair of seasoned dancers. Granny Dot clomped behind them in her rubber-soled shoes, chattering on about the cooling temperatures outside.

Madeline snagged Trey's arm as he moved to follow them down the hallway. "What's your rush?"

"But I . . . we have to hear what they're saying!" he hissed. "So we know what they know. So I don't trip up."

"Settle down. You'd have to make a huge blooper to get through to that guy right now."

"He's pretty shrewd, Mad. One wrong whiff of this fishy setup and he'll be through with Creative Works!"

Madeline took his leather jacket and headed for the entry closet. She tucked it away and turned back to find Trey hovering right behind her. She couldn't help smiling into his earnest brown eyes, darkened with panic to the shade of his chocolate-colored sweater. "This isn't a hard sell like one of your professional pitches. We don't have to convince Swain that we're married—he already believes it. All we have to do is keep up the bluff."

"Oh, is that all," he sarcastically fired back.

"Besides, this visit isn't about you or me, or your ad campaign, or even a family meal." She shook her head with amusement. "Somehow the priority here has totally escaped you."

"Oh yeah?" he said angrily. "The bottom line is getting his signature on the bottom line!"

Madeline laughed merrily. "Wake up! Swain is here to meet my mother. I'm sure he fully intends to sign on with Creative Works already."

"You think he engineered this visit just to get a closer look at Joanna?"

"Watching him home in on her the way he did leaves no doubt in my mind," she confirmed.

"Why, with all the women in California?" he wondered in bewilderment.

"Obviously my photos and stories intrigued him the other night. And I may have laid it on a little thick, because I know he's just her type." She held up a hand as he attempted to speak. "But believe me, I thought he might give her a call. Just take her to a show or something before he left town."

"Instead you've turned my business deal into a matchmaking sleep over!"

"For whom?" she couldn't resist asking coyly.

Trey could feel red heat scorching his cheeks. "You always take the long road, the bumpiest detour, Mad."

"You didn't seem to mind the ride all that much!" she returned. "All I see in Joanna and Swain is a pair of lonely people looking for a second chance at love. They know the odds are crummy at their age, what with extended families and stepchildren and loads of emotional baggage. That's why they leap at opportunity, take the long shot. Force an issue with blackmail, if need be. Just because you are so totally against matrimony doesn't—"

"I don't know what I think anymore!"

"Well, befuddlement is a beginning, anyway," she relented with strained patience. "As for our fantasy holiday here, please believe that a relaxed front will go a lot farther than a tense attempt to categorize everything everybody says. No matter what is said—or not said—one of us will be able to save the situation, turn it around in your favor."

"It's what we Clancys do best!" Peter piped up from behind them.

Madeline and Trey whirled to find the boys standing a few feet away, eavesdropping without shame.

"As long as Swain is occupied, you may as well show Trey where he's going to sleep," Madeline directed with a swift glance at her watch. "I have to run a quick errand for forgetful Two. He needs a baby gift for his secretary—tonight!"

"You're leaving me now?" Trey demanded, aghast.

"The boys will take good care of you," she assured him, reaching back into the closet for a boxy denim jacket and her roomy leather purse.

"But Swain will wonder—"

"Don't worry about appearances. I'll bring home a few things from the market to justify my trip." She paused to poke the solid breadth of his chest. "Just remember, it's all in the attitude."

Peter picked up the pair of suitcases as Madeline slipped through the door. "The poor, dopey girl," he murmured pityingly.

Trey followed the boys up the stairs. "Just what do you mean?"

Peter leaned against the oak railing with a sigh. "We both know attitude alone won't pull you through this mess, Five. We've got to have a man-to-man talk, pronto."

Man-to-man? Trey rolled his eyes. "Okay, lead the way."

Peter gave Trey a brief tour of the upper level of the roomy house so he would be familiar with the layout. They began in the yellow guest nook, which was crammed with bookcases, a sleeper sofa and a sewing machine. "Swain will stay in here," Peter announced, dropping the bag with the initials HS stamped on the handle.

"You're a very observant young man," Trey commented, visibly impressed.

"He's a genius," Benji piped up matter-of-factly.

"So I heard," Trey admitted. "Perhaps you'll make a good adman someday. I'm always on the lookout for new employees."

"A partnership would be more like it," Peter amended cheerfully. "I figure I'll be out of college by the time I'm twenty. So we've got eight years to hammer out a deal."

"I like a man who's sure of himself," he replied good-humoredly. The tour continued, Trey intently noting the location and color of everybody's room, and the all-important bathroom. Wouldn't want to be caught stumbling around for that in the middle of the night! Joanna and Granny Dot shared the sea foam green decor, and Mad's nest was white with pink rosebuds. They ended up in the last room at the end of the hallway. Benji flicked the wall switch and the overhead fixture lit up.

This had to be the boys' headquarters, with its masculine blue tones and splashes of red and black in the spreads and curtains. A single twin bed with a Barney throw pillow flanked the inner wall. Bunk beds stood against the opposite wall near the window facing the backyard.

"This top bunk is usually vacant," Peter explained, heaving Trey's bag up on the mattress. "Unless Granny Dot has a snoring fit. Then Mom comes in here to escape."

"I see," Trey murmured with a chuckle.

"Granny Dot doesn't think she snores, but she does," Benji told him earnestly.

"We taped her once just for fun," Peter added. "She's heard it, but doesn't believe it's her. Sometimes we play it for company. Think Swain would like to hear it?"

"No!" Trey erupted fervently. When they gazed at him in surprise and disappointment, he sought a diplomatic response. "Look, guys, I believe you Clancys are a real blast most of the time. But just for the next couple of days, maybe you could throttle back on your exuberance."

"What's that?" Benji wondered in a squeak.

"Five wants us to act dull, Benj," Peter interpreted. "And not argue, right?"

Trey nodded in relief. "Exactly. This whole deal is really stressful for me. And anything you can do to help will be really appreciated."

"We'll do our best," Peter promised. "Madeline's already drilled us on the rules. It's the finer points that need tuning up. Some of the specialized services Benj and I have come up with might interest you a lot."

"Make your pitch," Trey invited with a wave, leaning a hip against the dresser near the closet.

Peter cleared his throat. "Here goes. As I said downstairs, I think Madeline is wrong about the attitude thing. Even if Mom keeps Swain in some sort of lovey-dovey cloud the whole time, the guy is bound to do some thinking on his own."

"Agreed," Trey said with rising hopes. Allies. He had allies in the house of Mad!

"Now, the sleeping plan is to have you sneak off to bed after Swain does—allowing him to think you'll be going to Madeline's room with her. Something Granny Dot would never allow, by the way, even if you promised to sleep *under* the bed," he cautioned soberly. Trey nodded in solemn understanding and Peter continued.

"Granny Dot thinks Swain's going to wear himself out dodging my mother, that he's bound to get short-winded and collapse by the eleven-o'clock news." Peter tipped his white blond head in Trey's direction. "But we both know that he might not run at all! Mom's still foxy. And as Madeline said herself, he's come here just to meet her. Why, he might be up half the night, *playing canasta*," he said with significance. "A separate favor I've already done for you—read up on the game and coached Mom and everybody else on the finer points. We can easily run that bluff and any others that pop up."

Trey analyzed Peter's expectant look. "I take it you want me to hire you on as my troubleshooters."

"Yes," Peter promptly affirmed. "I'm saving up for new glasses and it's urgent!"

Trey pulled out his wallet. "To tell you the truth, I'm more than comfortable with the arrangement. Ten dollars for the canasta lesson?" When Peter nodded, he pulled out a bill and handed it over.

"Don't forget about me," Benji pleaded with a jutting lip.

"You're next, kid," Peter assured him, giving his brother's head a rub. "Benji can really add some motivation, some plausibility, to the sleeping arrangements," he told Trey. "Having you sneak around in your pajamas is too risky. It would be better if Swain knew you were in here with us, and for a logical reason. That way you could go to bed anytime. You might be the first soldier to fall with Madness chasing you around the house."

"Well . . ." Trey stroked his jaw, struggling to suppress the delightful vision.

"We won't blame ya for runnin'," Benji chirped. "We run from her, too, sometimes."

"We were thinking of a couple of ways to handle it," Peter said. "For instance, Benji throws a heck of a tantrum. He could do it for Swain's sake. Show 'em, Benj."

Benji hurled his small body to the carpet, feets and fists flailing. "I want Five in my rooom!" he whined on a high note surely dangerous to four-legged animals. "Tonight!"

Peter snapped his fingers, bringing a halt to the tirade. "What do you think?"

"Seems almost too dramatic," Trey objected thoughtfully.

"Yeah, it's a natural flaw in us," Peter explained. "Tend to go overboard at times."

"What else have you come up with?"

Before Trey knew what was happening, Benji had jumped to his feet and was charging him. Trey moved away from the dresser just as the little boy collided with his torso. He wrapped his small arms around him, burying his face in Trey's belly. "Be with us, please, oh, please, oh, please." His pleas continued for about ninety seconds. Trey found himself strangely moved by the cuddling child. He set an uncertain hand on the small, shaggy head. "Okay, tiger."

"Great response, Five!" Peter congratulated him. "That mixture of compassion and nervousness was just the right touch."

Trey took a quavering breath as Benji released him. Peter was shrewd, but not shrewd enough to know he hadn't been faking his response. He'd never been hugged by a child before, had never engaged in warm camaraderie with youngsters at all. The children sent by agencies for advertising work were distant and professional. These boys really seemed to like him. For some inexplicable reason, he found it gratifying. "Let's go with this second number," he declared over the lump in his throat.

"Good choice!" Peter cheered. "How does three dollars for Benji sound?"

Trey peeled off the bills and delivered them to the five-year-old now seated on his bed with his purple-and-green Barney pillow in his lap.

"You know Barney, Five?" Benji asked in a singsong voice.

"Of course. A smart adman keeps up with all creative phenomena."

Benji nodded in approval, hugging the pillow. "Good."

"I think I'd better go down to the kitchen now," Trey said with a glance at his watch. "Mad should be back soon." On a final note he added, "Please, fellas, try to call me Trey."

"We'll join you after a while... Trey," Peter said, testing the name as though it were totally foreign. "Putting Benji in his pajamas for the scene will add just the right homey feel. Don't you agree?"

Trey descended the stairs wearing something totally unexpected. A smile.

10

MADELINE RETURNED forty-five minutes later with a jug of milk and a pound of butter in her hands. She eased through the back door to find a small party in the kitchen. Trey, Swain and Joanna were seated at the round dinette table, laughing and murmuring as Swain's pipe smoke rose over their heads.

"Nobody missed me," she deduced with a good-humored pout.

"Finally, a foursome for our game!" Swain declared, greeting her heartily.

"Oh, good!" Joanna added pertly, her lush auburn hair swinging on her shoulders as she slipped out of her chair to join Madeline at the open refrigerator. Laying a hand on the sleeve of her daughter's denim coat, she spoke in a hushed voice. "Why on earth did you get more milk and butter?"

"Because I needed a cover for my trip to Two's place," Madeline replied in barely audible tones as she adjusted things on the shelves to accommodate the dairy additions.

"Another brew, guys?" Joanna called out sweetly over her shoulder.

"Yes!" they both responded, returning to their own conversation.

"What's all this about a game?" Madeline asked, digging cold bottles of beer out from behind a bowl of green salad. Joanna took them one by one, prying off the caps with an opener.

"Well, Trey has been watching Swain and me play two-handed canasta," she explained. "With you, we can play with four people in two teams."

"Darn good thing Peter taught us all," Madeline quipped dryly. With a measure of awe, she added, "You sound like you're enjoying the game as well as the man."

Joanna clasped her hands together almost gleefully. "The man is dishy and the game is divine! As sort of a hostess gift, Swain brought us a canasta set—two decks of cards with a lifetime finish in a tray of teak! A spinning tray of teak!"

"I never thought I'd hear you gushing on about cards," Madeline mumbled. "You sure it isn't just the dishy man bearing gifts who has your interest?"

"No! I'm so sorry I didn't shuffle my first deck years ago. Guess Granny Dot's stodgy bridge club gave me a negative impression. But cards can be fun. I plan to organize some sort of canasta club here in Tuckahoe next week."

Madeline's creamy features furrowed in concern over her impulsive mother's latest decision. "But what about your other interests? The crafty things you do so well?"

Joanna frowned slightly, then brightened in understanding. "I'll make time for everything—don't you fret."

"I might fret just a little bit," Madeline retorted, thumping the fridge door shut.

"I won't let you," Joanna protested gaily, peeling Madeline's jacket from her shoulders. Squeezing the denim in her hands, she cast a fond look toward the men chatting at the table. "Isn't that masculine music

wonderful? I've missed it so, especially at the holidays.
But having two nice male guests has brought back all
the poignant pleasures of mixed conversation. I've been
remembering how Thanksgiving Eve was when your
Dad was still here, when the men from the neighborhood used to drop by for some of our wine and a slice
of apple pie. Their wives won't let them come anymore...."

"Just goes to prove how attractive you still are,
Mom," Madeline said, consoling her. "Too dangerous
to entertain their husbands."

Joanna sighed in pensive agreement, hanging the
jacket on a hook by the door. "Can't break the Clancy
code now by expressing false modesty. I'm just too
tempting for my own good."

With a fit of giggles, the women took two beers each
and headed for the table. A loud, wheezing snort
pierced their laughter and the men's rumblings, causing a moment of startled silence.

"Oh, so that's where Granny Dot's gotten to,"
Madeline observed in clear tones, gazing beyond the
men into the sunken family room. The old woman was
sound asleep in the recliner, her head tipped back, her
mouth gaping open.

The others turned their attention to Granny. Trey's
jaw tightened as he attempted to read Swain's expression. The old lady had been going at it in stereo for
nearly half an hour. And to think he'd been concerned
about the boys playing a cassette! "She always this, uh,
restless?" he asked with a tinge of desperation.

"My mother-in-law is a woman with many facets,"
Joanna joked in obvious fondness. "It's best to just accept it and continue on with whatever."

Well said, Madeline thought, flashing a wan smile at the rapidly paling Trey. She'd done her best with the bunch, but some "real life" moments were bound to pierce this bubble of make-believe they were all swimming around in. "Clancy behavior does tend to be a bit erratic sometimes," she told Swain, setting a beer before him with a flutter of eyelashes.

"All families have their eccentricities," he said soothingly, tipping his bottle against Joanna's with a clink. "Here's to your health, lovely lady," he proclaimed, taking a healthy sip.

"Trey isn't accustomed to larger families ... yet," Madeline ventured, easing into a chair. "His was a lonely childhood, with no relatives and no stability."

Trey's gaze sharpened. He hadn't told her that! So how did she know? Vic? His heart slammed against his chest as he examined the situation. What could be more dangerous than a diva with inside information? A diva with motives, that's what! Her gaze had shifted from Swain to him now. The beguiling expression she'd favored the frozen-food king with had transformed into a seductive glint for his eyes only.

"Of course, it's never too late to get on the family track," Madeline purred, parting her mouth just a fraction as she raised her beer bottle.

"He has all the time in the world to learn the ins and outs of extended relationships." Swain favored Trey with a wink as he reached for the cards.

Trey's left eye twitched nervously. The old guy didn't know zip! Time? There was no time. Madeline had given him an ultimatum, if he recalled—make a realistic commitment or they were nowhere. And she was shifting levers right and left to make him squirm, to make him think, to make him feel. Yes, the fog was clearing. He was wise enough to realize that he was raw and vulnerable in this situation. She held all the aces before the first deal. This charade was for his benefit, but the household goddess—the all-knowing, all-consuming diva—was in control. And he'd begged and bullied his way into her Tuckahoe snare, filled with loose-tongued scrappers who would shake you upside down for your last dime, hugging you all the while.

Even through his veil of fear over losing this account, his uncertainty over the sacrament of matrimony, he wanted to bed her. Drive himself inside her over and over again until she shared his vulnerability. A deeper probe into her shimmery eyes convinced him just how far her plans had evolved. She may have not deliberately lured him and Swain here for the holiday, but she'd damn well decided to make the most of it, forcing him to see family and commitment in a new, desirous light. The reasoning behind her offer of unconditional help was sinking in now. She wanted him indebted to her emotionally. It could only mean one thing: she was grooming him for the real-life-husband slot invitingly open in her life. Vic had been right when he said Mad wanted to marry him!

And, dammit, sitting here in this atmosphere of caring and warmth, it did seem feasible. It was so flattering that of all the men she'd dated in the city, she wanted *him*. It could easily be the break of a lifetime to a man in the marrying mood, a man shrewd enough to recognize perfection. Madeline was the prototype wife; it was a simple, objective fact. He wasn't a whipped pup, as Vic claimed. He was a shrewd businessman who knew the art of making a sweet deal.

As Madeline watched Trey linger among his private thoughts, Benji raced in, wearing his superhero pajamas, complete with red cape. She inhaled sharply, sensing that something was up. Her curiosity deepened considerably when Trey shifted in his chair, pushing it away from the table a fraction. He wasn't the least bit surprised by Benji's arrival. And his color was back. He was the picture of rosy-cheeked expectation!

"The superhero has arrived!" Swain announced heartily, ruffling Benji's mop of pale hair. "Just like my oldest grandson. Always flying around in a play world."

Peter was on hand a moment later, with a look of exasperation beyond his years. "I tried to stop 'em, Mom."

Joanna's thin brows arched. "You did?"

"I mean, the kid is going nuts," Peter claimed. "I told him no ten times, but—"

"But I want Five in my room tonight!" With the patter of bare feet and a billowing cape, Benji flew into Trey's lap.

Swain stared at the man and boy in bewilderment. "Five? What's that mean?"

"Well, it's silly but simple," Madeline hastened to say, then paused noticeably. "You know Trey means 'the third' . . . Well, the boys think it's fun to call Trey Five," she offered lamely.

"You may even catch Granny Dot doing it," Joanna had the foresight to add.

Swain absorbed the explanation as another snort from Granny Dot echoed the length of the house. "My grandkids call me the king," he intimated with a shrug. "Would you like me to call you Five, too, Trey?"

"No!" Trey protested on a note of desperation.

"Now, you know that Madeline and Five are married," Peter went on to scold his brother with a wagging finger. "They belong together and that's that!"

Benji shook his head and burrowed into Trey's chest. "Don't care. Want Five in the up-high bunk. Might have a tantrummm," he warned in a familiar singsong tone, peeking out to gauge his audience's reaction.

"No, no, that won't be necessary," Trey said consolingly, rubbing the boy's back. "I'll bunk with you boys if you want me to. After all, Madeline has me all the time. Isn't that right, dear?" He bestowed a clothes-melting grin on her, eager to flex some of his sensual muscles, as well. She broke eye contact first in an obvious effort to collect her cool. It had to be a surprise to the mastermind, he decided, finding out that the troops were plotting their own strategies. Served her right for bailing out to please some other husband.

"Why don't we go tuck Benji in before the big canasta tournament, *dear?*" Madeline suggested lightly.

"Sure, go ahead," Swain encouraged them with a shooing hand. "We'll be fine."

Madeline nearly flew up the front staircase after the boys, but Trey managed to snag her around the waist as she passed the sewing nook. With a firm grip and a few steps, he managed to steer her into her own bedroom. He kicked the door shut after them, crowding her against the rosebud wallpaper. They were both heaving as he pinched her chin, tipping her face up to meet his.

"Having fun yet?" she asked in a rich, playful voice.

"No woman has ever dared push me to my limits the way you do," he growled softly, his thumb running down the tender column of her throat.

"Whatever do you mean?" she breathed.

"Luring me here to teach me lessons in love and marriage—"

"Allowing you to come so you could pawn me off as your wife," she corrected.

"Offering so-called free favors, so I'd be snagged on the biggest hook of all—"

"Trying to kick out the money crutch you lean so heavily upon." She frowned suddenly, giving his taut chest a sharp rap. "So just how much did the boys get out of you? And don't bother denying that a deal was hammered out. The performances were pretty convincing, but none of you are Broadway bound!"

"Just a few dollars changed hands," he assured her. "And I understand about the glasses. A closer look at Granny Dot during her snooze made everything clear."

"Yes, she made an issue of buying the same gold frames just to stir things up. Even claims she had them first, back in the forties. Poor Peter's a wreck over it."

"Can't your mother afford new glasses?" Trey asked in wonder, the answer seemingly simple in his mind.

"Dad worked for the railroad and his pension money only goes so far," Madeline replied, a mask falling over her features. "She manages, as we all manage. So I want this under-the-table money to stop!"

"If you want to be privy to every negotiation, you'll have to stick around, monitor my every move. How does that challenge sound, *wife?*" He began to move his hands, skimming them down her curves, then back up her hips and beneath her large sweater. When she released a sigh of pleasure, he pressed the length of his body into hers, his fingers climbing her rib cage. Lightning jolted his groin as the underside of her breast came to rest in his palm. Soft, heavy, bare to the touch. A graze of his thumb over her nipple drew it to a nubble of flesh.

She cried out in delighted surprise. "Now who's snagging who on a hook?"

"You court your way and I'll court mine," he uttered into her fragrant hair.

"You're taking unfair advantage of my weakness for your touch," she accused.

He groaned in satisfaction. "Why, dear, I had no idea I held any kind of advantage. I just assumed I'd take my licking and be done with it."

She stared back at him with a crazy, lopsided smile. "No, you didn't. You're in the mating game all right, Five. Scared as hell, but wondering if you could handle marriage after all. To me."

Trey straightened in disbelief and dropped his hand abruptly. Never before had he met a woman so straightforward, so cocky. "How can you be so certain, Mad? How do you know I'm not here just because of Swain?"

"Because there's a hell of an energy between us. Because you're being impossibly territorial about my other husbands. Because you've copped a feel at first opportunity."

Trey exhaled what felt like a lungful of steam. "Vic called you, didn't he?"

"Yes," she lightly affirmed, skimming his jawline with her fingernail. "He wanted to make sure I knew this was more than just another free-lance job. And to double-check on my intentions, find out if I'd given up on you. He seems to think you've come to me as fragile as a whipped pup."

"He loves that term, the rat!"

"He's this pup's best friend!" she teased, tweaking Trey's nose. "And he's wise enough to see that your hard-line approach could drive a woman away."

"You don't seem to be fleeing."

Her eyes danced with mischief. "You've finally met your match, mister. If I can't make a legally tendered husband out of you, nobody can."

Her frankness gave him the courage to say what he yearned to say. "Mad, I've been living on a roller coaster ever since we made love. I'm smart enough to know that I am in love with you. In love in a way that tells me I've never really been in love before."

"Smile when you say that," she coaxed.

Trey's mouth curved wolfishly.

"Not that kind of smile!" she protested.

"A man makes the most gallant gesture imaginable, and you complain about his mouth?" Trey taunted.

Mad was about to argue that that sort of look had only one consummate cure when she saw a twinge of teasing in his eyes. Standing on tiptoe, she rubbed her hands over the taut muscles of his chest. "Welcome to love, my darling. I know we'll make each other blissfully happy."

"Me, happy as your home-base husband?" His face clouded in trepidation.

"Trey, those other men mean nothing to me. If they did, I wouldn't have been searching the city for a mate. And I certainly wouldn't have, uh, tried a tango or two."

"I came to that same conclusion," he confessed. "Still, your job is demanding. Caregiving is a tremendous drain. Multiply it by five—plus me—and I just don't see how you could manage."

"The job suits me perfectly," she insisted.

"I know it does," he said between gritted teeth. "You're so damn right for it that I want you to be my lawfully wedded wife. All mine, forever and ever."

Their eyes locked in a long, startled moment of joy.

"Love and marriage in the same conversation?"

Trey nodded. "I'm happy to announce that, after you and Vic, I am the third person to make the discovery. Hopefully ahead of Eddie, Gina and Martin the doorman."

"Oh, Trey!"

"Well, it's true, isn't it? At least you two knew my fate ahead of me." He gripped her chin lightly in his fingers. "Now that you know I'm playing for keeps, maybe you can bend a little. Consider another career avenue."

Her forehead furrowed in worry. "Job changes require money, careful planning. And I really like my freedom, Trey. I'm busy, but I can restructure my schedule. And I frequently have the chance to stretch myself, exercise my ingenuity. I cherish those perks."

"Put yourself in my place, honey," he suggested. "Would you like me playing butler to five women, being on call to them day and night?" With satisfaction, he watched the play of emotion cross her features.

"Well, I admit you've got me there."

His dark eyes gleamed knowingly. "Uh-huh."

A series of sharp, rapid knocks on the door interrupted them.

"You comin' to tuck me in or not?" Benji demanded in a muffled whine.

"Yes, we're coming," Trey called out.

"I'll think things over," she promised.

He reached for the doorknob, then turned back with a small smile. "I want you and your family to know that I appreciate the effort you're putting in on my behalf."

"Just investing in my own future," she assured him with a twinkle.

"Wish you could help me through the night," he said, with a wistful glance at the fluffy, eyelet-covered bed. "The whole night this time."

She sighed in regret. "Sorry, husband. The Clancys aren't that gung ho on Method acting."

"C'mon, Five!" Benji urged, delivering another blow to the door.

"Back to the stage for us," Trey said with mock drama, whisking it open.

TREY AWOKE THANKSGIVING morning as the sun slanted through the window onto his top bunk. He struggled to sit up, surveying the room with a huge yawn. The boys' beds were already empty and neatly made. The clown clock on the dresser read half past seven.

It was an embarrassingly late start for a sunrise jogger—and he was still tired! No wonder, really, considering the troubled night he'd spent, plagued with images of Mad in a flowing pink nightgown and flowing golden hair, twirling below his bunk in a soft vision of cotton candy and apricots. Creative Works gone mad! It was the curse of an active imagination.

With thoughts of an invigorating run through the neighborhood, Trey swiftly eased into his gray sweats and headed to the bathroom for a quick shave, trying not to count the new lines around his dark eyes. The next stop would be Mad's room for a brief rundown on her day. He'd never cared much for surprises, even as a child. *Especially* as a child! It usually meant a new man in his mother's life or a new home. The idea of surprises being hurled at him hour after hour all day long made him quake in his running shoes.

The question of whether or not to knock was answered by Madeline's open door. The room was exactly as he'd left it last night, except for the candy pink nightgown draped over the Queen Anne chair near the window. He couldn't resist the temptation to step up to examine it, to see if it was indeed the same gown of his dreams. The fabric slid over his fingertips like a silky waterfall, convincing him that it was. What had she been doing in the boys' room after midnight? The card tournament hadn't ended until eleven forty-five. He and Swain had indulged in one final beer while Mad and Joanna had rinsed some stray dishes. Then the two men had retired together, leaving the women in the kitchen to rouse Granny Dot and steer her upstairs.

The gown settled back onto the chair as Trey stared blankly out the second-story window, searching internally for answers. He found his eyes riveted to a sight on the opposite side of the street. It was Mad, dressed in a scarlet outfit. With Benji's help, she was tugging along a loaded coaster wagon. It was obviously the boy's job to trot alongside and keep the cargo steady. Trey pushed aside the wispy ruffle of rosebud-covered curtain, pressing his nose against the pane for a better view. The wagon was packed solid, with what appeared to be a roaster dominating the center. Meals on wheels? For a Tuckahoe husband, no doubt! Jealousy engulfed him until he felt his blood flow green. There had to be an easy out of this excruciating predicament.

Perhaps it was the trauma, perhaps it was just his muse catching up with him, but a resolution suddenly popped into his head. And it was so simple, Trey couldn't believe he'd overlooked it until now. Madeline could put her talents to use at Creative Works. She was quick-witted, ambitious and charming. And she'd still have the flexible hours she preferred. He would pitch the campaign to her as soon as time allowed. But for now there was Swain to think about. Did he know about this movable feast? Trey tore out of the room to find out.

Savory smells wafted through the Clancy kitchen despite the early hour. Trey wasn't very familiar with how turkey dinners were prepared—his mother had never tackled a bird herself—but it made sense that the preparation would take some time.

Granny Dot was standing at the stove, stirring a kettle of something with a big wooden spoon. Dressed in a pale blue housedress, her hair neatly rolled, she looked rested and on top of things. Just the authority figure to speak to.

"Morning, Five," she greeted him heartily.

"Good morning." With his hands clasped behind his back, he sidled up behind her.

She turned to survey him with a cluck of her tongue. "You look tense, son. With everything running so smoothly, too. Under Madeline's watchful eye, I mean," she added. "Turkey's roasting, cranberries here are bubbling." She reached into a drawer beneath the counter and rattled through the silverware inside.

Dipping a teaspoon into the steaming red sauce, she held it up to his mouth. "Here now—have a taste."

"No, thank you—"

She patted his cheek with a wrinkled hand. "Mind your manners now. Eat!"

"Hot," he squawked as the sauce nipped his lip.

"Blow on it!" she directed, squeezing his mouth to an O. "Didn't your mother give you tastes when you were a boy?"

"No," he said through his contorted mouth. "She worked long hours and opened a lot of cans."

"I'm sure her feet were too tired from hairstyling all day to stand at the stove at night," Granny Dot conceded understandingly.

"How did you know?" he asked through his hollowed mouth.

"Somebody told me," she said, finally relinquishing her grip on his face. "Peter or somebody."

"How would *he* know, Dot?" Trey asked in bewilderment, taking the teaspoon she thrust into his hand.

"Granny Dot to you, young fella," she corrected succinctly, returning to her kettle to stir the simmering sauce. "Only men over sixty may take such a liberty. Must've been Madeline who told me about your mother," she amended. "You must have told her."

This certainly was a package deal. Not only had Madeline seeped into his every pore, but she'd brought the whole Clancy clan along. He didn't recall telling Mad about his mother's profession. But no matter, Swain was the focus right now.

"Granny Dot," he began again on a frantic note, "I just spotted Madeline on the street with a wagon and a roaster!"

"Dinner for One," she promptly replied. "Not one person, mind you. But for husband One." She sighed in reminiscence. "He was her first, you know. The one who began it all. Who'd have guessed that single housekeeping job would evolve into Just Like a Wife? One's parents had decided to move to Arizona, for the old man's arthritis, so they say. The son didn't want to move along, not with his bookkeeping job at the meat packers going so well. They advertised for a caregiving maid, and Madeline applied. Could've been a romantic match, if he weren't such a frail mama's boy," she confided with a *tsk*. "You know the type. Well, he's been on pins and needles the last few weeks because the folks were returning for the holiday. Paid handsomely for this extra meal."

"How was this turn of events explained to Swain?" Trey anxiously broke in to ask.

Granny Dot heaved her ample bosom. "'Twasn't to my knowledge. I helped Madeline load the wagon all by myself."

"Where is Swain now? I know he's not sleeping, I checked."

"You're the last to rise, all right," she confirmed with a judgmental *humph*. "You a late riser by habit, Five?"

Trey clenched his teeth, noting that there seemed to be a pattern of giving all the husbands labels—identifying tags. One was frail, Two was forgetful and he was a potential sleepyhead! They'd make a great Disney movie: *Sheer Madness and the Five Husbands*. "Actually, I'm an early riser," he hastened to assure her. "It just so happens I had a restless, uncomfortable night."

Granny Dot pursed her lips. "Odd. That mattress is like new. Rarely used at all."

Trey gave a grim smile. *Occupied only on the odd evening when your snoring drives Joanna to a more peaceful haven.*

"You should be sleeping like a baby, Five," she insisted as he ate the spoonful of tart sauce and moved to set the teaspoon in the sink. "We'll take good care of you, as though you were still an official husband."

Somehow, the reassurance was comforting and frightening at the same time. But the cranberries were good, as the meal would no doubt be. Madeline must've cooked her heart out.

"Perhaps Peter has seen Swain." Granny Dot sidled over to open the basement door. "Peter!" Her blaring tones echoed down the stairwell.

A door opened somewhere below, and Peter appeared at the bottom of the steps, looking rather ragged dressed in his pajama top and jeans. "I said I was not to be disturbed! You know I—" He stopped in midsentence when Trey joined Granny Dot in the doorway. "Oh, hello, Five. Finally rolled out of the sack, I see."

"What are you doing down there?" Trey asked, busting with curiosity.

He shrugged his thin shoulders. "Just messing around with Mad's computer."

The twelve-year-old seemed a bit uneasy, and Trey couldn't help but wonder about it. Mad seemed to carry such weight around the house, when no one else seemed especially hardworking. What a waste for the boy to be whiling away the hours with games when he could be pitching in. Surely he would've been more of a help to Mad with the wagon than little Benji.

"Five is looking for Swain," Granny Dot explained. "Have you seen him?"

Peter sighed with exasperation, and with what appeared to be relief. "Mom took him for a stroll about an hour ago to get him out of the way for the wagon train, if that's what's worrying you." A grin split the boy's face. "If you don't mind, I'm kinda busy." He disappeared again, a door closing below.

Granny Dot clapped her hands together. "So there you are! Nothing to fear."

There was nothing *but* fear when one was doling out lies, forced to rely upon a cross between the wild bunch and the Brady Bunch to make them stick.

"I believe I'll go for my jog," he said, hoping to shake off his head-to-toe jangle.

"Yes, you go on out and play. We'll handle things. It's what you're paying us for."

Trey barreled out the back door with clenched fists. The entire family must believe they were on salary for this one! The bunch of operators. So accustomed to seeing Mad paid for her wifely services, they were all expecting to share in the profits for this performance.

Trey was beginning to suspect strongly that Mad was supporting the lot of them. It certainly explained her commitment to her current job, why she was reluctant to take some time to shop around for a different position. The Clancy empire would no doubt crumble without the husbands' weekly paychecks. He would help her out of her dilemma. Surprise her with *his* insight and ingenuity, for a change!

11

TREY JOGGED OUT INTO the brisk morning in pursuit of Madeline, rounding the house on the dewy grass to the sidewalk fronting the old, middle-class homes. She'd progressed little more than a block during his encounter with Dot, and was in the process of turning the corner.

Benji, in his navy hooded sweatshirt, spotted him first and put a detaining hand on his sister's arm. Madeline was just spinning around when Trey caught up with them.

"What do you think you're doing out here?" she demanded, squinting up at him against the bright sky.

"Jogging."

"Oh, sure," she said dubiously. "Checking up on me is more like it."

"Granny Dot already explained about your trip, Little Red Riding Hood," he teased with a tug at her scarlet velour top.

"You must be the Big Bad Wolf!" Benji piped up.

"Right you are." Trey bared his teeth with a growl. Madeline actually flinched a little. The sight was a sweet one. She was just too sure of herself too much of the time.

"I hope you aren't planning to stop me," she said haltingly, gripping the handle of the wagon a little harder.

Trey looked down into the wagon for the first time. Just as he'd figured, there was a huge roaster in the center. Other pots and bowls were wedged around it, the works insulated with rolled-up towels. Was there no order she couldn't fill? The woman was a corporation in herself! "I'm not going to try and stop you from doing your job," he assured her earnestly, "catering to that fragile mama's boy. I just wanted to help you along, shave the odds of you running into Swain and your mother."

"Tough luck, Five," Benji squeaked. "Here they come now."

"If you hadn't stalled us, we would've made it around the corner and out of sight," Madeline grumbled. "Right, Benj?"

Benji's hooded head bobbed up and down. "Yup."

"If either of you has ever thought of trying a moment of silence, this would be a good time," Trey cautioned with a fortifying breath.

"Before you get too creative, I'd check out what Mom has told him," she advised.

"Hello there!" Joanna hailed them cheerily. She flashed them an apologetic look as Swain bent over to inspect the wagon.

"You kids aren't planning a picnic, are you?" he asked with a quick, inquisitive peek underneath the black roaster cover.

"I hadn't thought of that!" Joanna blurted out, clasping her own windswept cheeks.

Trey groaned inside. These Clancys had so little control over their tongues. And Joanna's growing infatuation with the frozen-food king was only bound to make her performance weaker. For a man who was accustomed to being at the helm of all dealings relating to business, this was the severest of torture.

"I take it Mom didn't explain," Madeline said on a querying note.

"Not yet," Swain said, straightening up to give Joanna's nose a tweak. "It's so darn cute the way she jumps from subject to subject."

Trey leapt ahead to fill in the blanks. "Well, Madeline happens to be—"

"Helping a frail friend, is all Joanna said," Swain interrupted with a casual shrug.

Madeline shot Trey an I-told-you-to-wait look.

Trey sighed in resignation. Mad had been right about caution. But he'd been right about the tags. They all called One frail. And Two forgetful. Well, he would not be known as sleepyhead! He couldn't help but wonder what tags they already had for him.

"You must let us help you," Swain insisted, reaching out for the wagon's handle.

"Oh, no," Madeline declined smoothly. "He's terribly shy. Won't even want Trey to come along."

"That's right, darling," Joanna cooed, slipping her arm through Swain's. The "darling" was not missed by Trey or Madeline, who exchanged a meaningful look. "Let's go back to the house for a nice cup of coffee."

"Take Trey with you," Madeline suggested. "I believe he's totally lost in those moments when I am off doing other things."

"Don't like to share this lady," Trey agreed heartily, planting a kiss on Madeline's fragrant temple. "It's unbearable," he whispered to her alone, his eyes intense with emotion.

Madeline smiled at him, a hundred-watter to rival the sun. His butler analogy had illustrated his point all too vividly. She couldn't stop thinking about how she'd hate to be in his shoes. There had to be some sort of compromise to remedy the situation, but it was more complicated than Trey knew. There were things he didn't yet understand. She was hit with the sudden impulse to run away with him and the wagon, have a picnic together in the park. She couldn't help but blink at him yearningly.

And Trey yearned right back at her. How could such a perfect woman exist in such an imperfect world? he wondered. She was nothing less than a marvel. Despite the fact that she lived at home, she was an independent woman of means. Not only was she balancing the demands of five husbands, she was supporting her family. No matter how endearing, no matter how loving, Trey could not believe how thoroughly they took her for granted, relied upon her talents and energies to carry the financial load. Pensions didn't support a household like theirs, even if both widows had one. No wonder Mad had been so evasive last night when he'd wondered why Peter couldn't have new glasses immediately. There just wasn't enough petty cash.

"You coming, Trey?" Swain asked, breaking into his thoughts.

Trey tore his gaze from Madeline. "No, I believe I'll go for a run."

"Never would've pegged you for a jogger," Joanna commented. "Sleepyhead."

Trey threw up his hands as he began to back away from them in a trot. "I'm not a sleepyhead! Please believe that!"

He had no contact with any of them until noon, when he descended the stairs, showered and dressed for the Thanksgiving feast. He froze in the entryway as feminine voices, lifted in obvious disagreement, drifted from the direction of the dining room. He moved swiftly through the living room to track down the trouble.

The large rectangular table in the dining area was covered in white linen and elegantly set with fine crystal and china. Madeline and Joanna, dressed in similar shantung dresses, were standing at the nearby buffet, bickering over a half-full vase of flowers and a potted mum. The buffet was littered with flowers, a florist's scissors and a smattering of leaves and stem pieces. The women obviously hadn't heard his footsteps on the plush beige carpet, for they didn't give him as much as a glance.

"I told you I would take care of the centerpiece!" Joanna said.

"But you didn't, Mom!"

"The mums will be fine for the table."

"But I thought we agreed on cut flowers—"

"The time-efficient choice is the mum plant, Madeline!"

"If you'd spent less time with Swain and more time on this dinner—"

"What's the matter?" Trey interrupted anxiously, rushing up between them.

Madeline, her face nearly as white as her dress, whirled sharply at the sound of his voice. "Nothing. Nothing important. Tensions always run high around here right before a big meal like this."

"Everything's been so smooth up till now," Trey fretted, running a shaky hand through his damp hair. He'd handled many a disagreement between female employees, but these Clancy women did crazy things

to his nervous system. He didn't know where to begin....

"Surely Madeline told you we bicker a bit," Joanna
remarked matter-of-factly.

"Where is Swain?" he inquired tensely.

"Drove Benji down to the In 'n' Out for some vanilla
ice cream to go with the apple pie," Madeline reported
with forced brightness.

"If you'd gotten ice cream last night instead of milk
and butter, he wouldn't have had to go!" Joanna chided,
pressing the pink foil around the plant pot.

"Mom, I think he wanted the chance to drive our
Camaro," Madeline shot back.

"You know, Joanna," Trey said carefully, "Madeline
is doing her level best to make all of this fly."

Joanna's hazel eyes flashed dangerously. "Is that so?"

He knew he was deepening the controversy by entering the fray, but the injustices leveled on Madeline
were too much to ignore. Good sense and his healthy
fear of dangerous women signaled him to shut his
mouth, but her plight had been simmering in his
thoughts all morning, just as the cranberries bubbled
on the stove. "It would seem to me that if Madeline
wishes to take the time to do one of her wonderful floral arrangements, you should let her."

"What?" Joanna gasped indignantly. "Why, I—"

"I would really prefer it, if you don't mind," he went
on calmly but firmly. "Swain praised the one she left in
my apartment, and I think he'd appreciate it."

Joanna drew an incensed breath. "I think if I plopped
a jarful of weeds on the table he'd be content enough!
You don't have to have every little thing perfect for him.
He is just a man. A man who's come to see me!"

Granny Dot and Peter appeared in the kitchen door, their faces full of curiosity.

"A man who's still holding out his signature on my contract," Trey proclaimed, setting the paperwork in question atop some magazines on the end of the buffet. "That was the whole idea of this visit—to get his baby-food account!"

"I know that!" Joanna flounced by to set the potted plant on the table.

"I'm willing to pay whatever price," he assured them, a desperate edge in his voice.

"Trey!" Madeline protested in dismay.

"I'm sure whatever fee Madeline set is fine," Granny Dot put in, looking rather perplexed by the triangular duel in progress.

"Madeline had insisted that this job be a favor—"

Gasps of horror pierced the air.

He held up a hand to quell the rioting crowd. "And as much as I appreciate the sentiment, I'm more than willing to renegotiate." Under Mad's glaring disapproval, he added, "Consider it hush money, a bribe to guarantee your continued graciousness."

Another rumble made its way through the crowd.

"Trey, I wish you'd stop," Madeline pleaded. "This isn't the time or the place."

"Yes, it is, Mad," he said with perseverance. "I'm not about to judge the way you folks live," he went on reassuringly. "Every family has its way. But I have a stake in this for a few reasons—because of this free-lance job, because I was one of Madeline's client husbands, but most importantly, because I've fallen in love with her."

"Tell us something we don't know," Peter quipped with a triumphant look shared by Joanna and Granny Dot.

"All right," Trey obliged sternly. "I'm onto your system here—"

"Trey, don't!" Madeline begged desperately.

"Madeline is a gem, a wonder!" Trey raved lavishly. "The perfect wife, the perfect woman. Haven't any of you noticed?"

"We love and appreciate our Madeline!" Granny Dot bellowed in outrage.

"Let him continue," Joanna advised with narrowed brows. "I want to hear this. Tell us about our system, Five."

"I have no doubt that you have a loving home here," he reiterated, "but it seems criminal to me that Madeline has to support you all!" There, he'd said it. With heart-pounding expectation, he waited for their reaction.

"How preposterous!" Granny Dot fumed. "I have always carried my weight."

"All I've seen is Madeline working her tail off," Trey argued. "She was even the one who tiptoed into the boys' room last night to check on them."

"But, Trey," Madeline broke in, "you don't—"

"Even her office isn't sacred ground," he continued. "I imagine it's the hub of her business, the place where she does all of her scheduling and phoning. But I caught Peter messing around down there this morning. When he could've been helping her lug that wagon down to One's," he said with a chiding glance at the boy. "Sure, Granny Dot did her the favor of stirring the pot she left on the burner. And Joanna dazzled Swain while Madeline supplied a second turkey dinner to somebody. You all seem to rely so heavily on her lead and her financial resources. Why, when I look back at how she was forced to swallow her pride and come to my office to niggle her job back—"

"I didn't niggle," Madeline assured all of them.

"The desperation that must have fueled such an attempt boggles the mind!"

"I wanted your place back so I could use it in my husband search," Madeline frantically emphasized. "It was a selfish move that had nothing to do with my family!"

"Even now she's covering for you," Trey marveled. "Isn't she just too much?"

"Too much," Peter sniped.

"What I want to do is lift some of Madeline's load from her shoulders immediately," Trey explained. "I think she would be a huge asset to Creative Works. She could start immediately, with a generous salary. Perhaps not enough to support all of you, but a little juggling and duty delegation should easily turn this arrangement around. It's time for Madeline to have a life of her own, with me."

"Is this a marriage proposal, I do indeed hope?" Granny Dot inquired haughtily.

"Yes, I've already proposed. Last night, as a matter of fact," he told the slack-jawed crowd. "Now I'm offering her an invitation to share all that is mine, to join me in my business."

For a moment the Clancys were struck speechless.

"I wish you would've discussed this with me first," Madeline whispered fiercely, clutching his arm.

"I was going to, but watching this tussle over the flowers was the last straw," he returned quietly, as though they were suddenly alone. But they weren't. They still had a very roused, bit chomping audience.

"If everybody keeps their tempers, we can get through this dinner as planned," Madeline proposed in a strained voice, wringing her hands.

"I will murder anyone who wrecks this celebration for Swain and me," Joanna cautioned with a pouty look. "We must resist the temptation to stuff Five into a giant roaster and—"

"Mother!" Madeline gasped in consternation. Joanna bit her lip without apology. "It's my fault Trey feels the way he does about all of you," Madeline said placatingly. "Please don't take it out on him."

"Madeline!" Trey objected, openly appalled.

All the Clancys' eyes were on Madeline, as though she had the final say. The thump of car doors from the driveway punctuated the urgency of her decision.

"I can't settle this to everybody's satisfaction in a split second!" she wailed.

"You'd better decide what you do want, dear," Joanna advised. "About Five, about everything. We'll keep up the jolly in-law pretense. But no more lies about us. Five wants us to own up to our actions, and that is just what we are going to do!"

Everyone began to drift into the kitchen as Swain and Benji barreled through the back door with ruddy, happy faces.

A tug at this oxford shirt drew Trey to a halt near the buffet. He turned to find Peter at his elbow. "What is it?"

"Look, Five," he said under his breath, with one eye on the laughter-filled kitchen. "You're in a real pressure cooker now, pal."

"So I figured," he retorted dryly. "I hope you weren't offended by what I said."

"Hey, I understand you're duped silly by Madness. And I want to continue on with our private agreement. You know—help for a price."

"Sure, sure," Trey said with an encouraging wave. "What's on your mind?"

"An update and a plan," Peter whispered. "Not only do the Clancy women want to roast you for the turkey you are, but you've got Swain trouble. I overheard him on the phone this morning. His youngest daughter felt bad when she learned he had to cancel his trip to the oldest daughter's house in Ohio, so she's flying in to L.A. for the weekend just to be with her daddy."

Trey's jaw tightened. "When is he leaving New York?"

"This afternoon. I see you have the contract handy on the buffet. Smart move. I wouldn't be surprised if he's forgotten all about it, with Mom working on him."

"I've got to get him back on track," Trey mused.

"It'll be a cinch with my help," Peter assured him.

Trey gripped the boy's bony shoulders. "Kid, you help me get that signature, I'll buy those new glasses for you myself. Two pairs if you make it by dessert and coffee!"

"We'll need Benj . . ." he promptly bartered.

Trey snapped his fingers. "A pair of specs for Benj, too!"

"Doesn't wear 'em. But a Barney toy would do the trick," Peter bartered. "It would mean so much more to him than money."

"A true wheeler-dealer," Trey commended, offering his hand to shake on the deal.

TREY HAD NEVER CARVED a turkey, so he was more than delighted to bow to Swain's expertise. While Swain and Joanna worked with the roasted bird on the counter,

Trey tackled the job of mashing the potatoes on the table. He rolled up the sleeves of his pale blue oxford shirt, plunging the masher into the pot over and over again while Granny Dot delivered a thin stream of milk.

"Such strong muscles, son," Granny Dot cooed with a flash of humor.

Trey mashed on with a concessionary smile. They were going to pile it on now, under Swain's unassuming nose. Much in the same way Mad had done at the Four Seasons. Was it worth marrying into this sort of lunacy? It was! Madeline was his dream come true.

"So, tell me, Madeline," Swain said, pausing in his work, the huge knife poised in the air, "do you have any of your delicious house wine on tap?"

Madeline, in the process of digging the green salad out of the refrigerator for Benji's waiting hands, peeked over the door. "Why, of course."

"I can't quite place the flavor, but it is familiar," he mused in pleasure. "Something from way back...." He turned to Trey at the table. "Help me out, Trey."

Trey gawked at the wealthy frozen-food mogul, who was looking surprisingly domestic with a terry apron tied around his neck. "Guess I've just taken Madeline's wine for granted," he said. "One of the things she does so well."

"No reason to keep you fellows guessing any longer," Granny Dot announced briskly. She capped the jug of milk and passed it to Mad at the fridge. "Let's just take a tour through our wine cellar!"

Madeline gasped in dismay, smacking the fridge door shut. "Now, Granny Dot, a wine cellar to a man like Swain implies something altogether different—"

"How different can it be?" Swain objected, removing the apron from his neck.

"Well, I imagine it doesn't have an alarm system," Trey put in, tugging at the knot of his tie. He stole an anxious look at Mad. Wine cellar? The pinch of fear between her brows didn't comfort him any.

Granny Dot led the procession down the steep stairs to the basement. She veered left, to the laundry area with washer, dryer and clothesline. Trey, bringing up the rear, stole a peek into Madeline's office. Unlike the rest of the basement, it was partially finished, the concrete blocks painted a tranquil aqua, two high windows fringed with simple plaid curtains, a large area rug on the concrete floor. Just as he suspected, it was rigged with a handsome computer and fax machine. There were all sorts of charts propped up on easels, and bulletin boards lined the waist-high concrete ledge running the length of the outer wall. Everything was labeled One through Five.

Before he could get a closer look, Mad's voice sliced through him. "What on earth are you doing?"

Trey whirled to find her in the doorway, a lovely, furious cloud of white in her lush shantung dress.

"Get out of here before Swain sees!" she ordered fiercely.

His dark eyes grew round. Good lord, she was right! What had he been thinking of? He swiftly raced out of the room. She whisked the door shut, but not before, Trey noted, pushing in the button on the inside knob to lock it.

"Come along," she whispered. "Though I wish you didn't have to. . . ."

The Clancy wine cellar proved to be a small room beyond the laundry area. There was a workbench complete with tools, and a fancy table saw, leading Trey to believe that Madeline's father must have considered this his domain at one time. Then there was the wine operation. Trey gulped as he took in the sight. This was no ordinary cellar boasting racks full of vintage bottles. It was a wine-making setup. Of the crudest form, with glass gallon jugs full of fermenting juices, each topped with a huge colorful balloon in various stages of inflation. Beside the workbench was another bench, boasting corks, funnels, spoons, tubes, a balance and a variety of bottled chemicals.

"Oh, there you are, Trey!" Swain said from a squatting position near the bottles. "I haven't seen a homemade wine operation like this since I was a boy. Who'd have ever guessed the Clancy wine was dandelion!"

"Dan—dan—" Trey looked to Madeline for verification. She shrugged with an impish look. The wine she was passing off to her trendy businessmen husbands was derived from the yellow flower every lawn owner in America worked to eliminate! How ironic, how clever, how downright sneaky.

"We comb the neighborhoods every spring for just the right flowers," Granny Dot proudly expounded. "Then, under my supervision, the wine-making process is carried out. Mind you, only blossoms the size of the top half of my thumb are used." She paused to show both Swain, who'd risen to his feet, and Trey, who nearly sunk into the floor, the measure on her thumb. "The wine we're drinking now, of course, was made over a year ago. This batch won't be ready until after Christmas."

"How intriguing!" Swain enthused.

"I'm sorry if you expected some sort of fancy cellar," Madeline told him.

"Nonsense! Brings me back to my childhood, when my parents made the stuff. No wonder it made me feel so good!"

Trey and Madeline exchanged a look of relief. Granny Dot's move to be herself had only enhanced the Clancy image in Swain's eyes.

"Well, let's go eat!" Joanna suggested, clapping her hands together. "And have a little nip of dandelion, as well."

Trey and Madeline lingered as the others marched toward the stairs.

"I hope you're not too disappointed that the wine isn't from some chic Manhattan shop," Madeline said.

"Amazing what a little fancy packaging can do to the plain old truth," he marveled with a trace of chagrin in his voice.

"The basic technique of your average adman," she tossed back.

"Touché, Mad," he conceded. Then, burying his face in her hair, he said, "Luckily, I'm always on the lookout for inspired technique."

"Mmm . . . So you're really not angry?"

"No," he murmured into the curve of her ear. "Just as long as we share our trade secrets from now on. I love to have the inside track on my closest confidants inside and outside the business. I hate surprises."

"You hate them?" she echoed.

"Despise them," he purred.

"About the things you said to everybody," she whispered haltingly. "I may not be as perfect as you think. May not be able to just ease into your company."

"One look into that office of yours confirmed everything I said about your capabilities," he soothed. "I want you to think about my offer. Give up this husband business and become a creative consultant for me."

"I don't have a college degree," she protested. "I was a checker in a Tuckahoe supermarket before I started up Just Like A Wife. It was a part-time business with just one husband at first, income to supplement things after my father died."

"Nobody could've done a better job creating a business!" he complimented. "Do you know how many people with years of education fail because they don't have the nerve and savvy to keep things alive?" He set his hands on her hips and drew her closer. "Mad, I am totally in love with you. But I cannot deal with being a fifth or sixth wheel in your schedule. No matter how you might try to balance us all, it would never be enough for me. I want to be the only husband in your life." With his face inches from hers, he skimmed her features. "I don't expect these changes to happen overnight, but you can set the wheels turning. I will be more than happy to help you out financially. All of you. Promise me you'll consider everything I've said."

"It's already all I can think about," she confided.

He was about to kiss her when he felt another presence nearby.

"You guys better get a move on," Peter announced, pushing his glasses up his nose. "Dinner's ready and Granny Dot's stalling with the longest premeal prayer in Clancy history."

Trey sighed with pleasure. This was all going to work out. For the first time, he had a grip on Mad and a grip on the Swain account. It didn't feel like Thanksgiving. It felt like Christmas!

IT WAS DESSERT TIME before the boys put their contract-signing scam into action. Benji was the designated brother. He sidled up to Swain's chair just as Madeline was doling out pie à la mode, with Trey trailing behind, serving coffee.

"You gonna hire my big brother?" Benji chirped, winding his thin arm around Swain's shoulders. Swain turned in his chair to regard Benji in confusion. "Hire Peter for what?"

"I mean Five," he corrected with a toothy smile.

"We're already in the thick of things," Swain assured him. Trey set the coffeepot down on the table and slipped back into his chair beside the frozen-food king. With a broad smile, Swain reached over to dump three sugar cubes into Trey's steaming cup. "I know how you like your sugar," he said jovially. "And today is no time to cut back."

"Plenty of time for dieting tomorrow," Trey agreed, wincing at the syrupy brew.

"Benj and I are fascinated by contracts," Peter piped up, taking Trey's contract from the buffet. "The here-tos and wherefores are totally cool." He stepped in between Trey and Swain and unfolded the papers on the tablecloth. Trey noted that Benji was rubbing Swain's back now with his small hand. "I expect to be working with Five one day," Peter informed him with a thrust to his thin chest. "Partners."

Swain chuckled, digging his fork into his pie. "Wonderful pie."

"Peter was telling me you're leaving early, Swain," Trey pressed, intent on keeping the focus on business.

Swain swallowed, dabbing his mouth with his napkin. "Yes. My youngest is flying home for the weekend. Insisted, actually. So I'm leaving later on this afternoon."

"Granny Dot and I are driving him to the airport," Joanna took obvious pleasure in reporting. "Didn't anyone mention it to you, dear?"

"No, they did not," Trey returned levelly. "Swain and I have barely touched base. And talked nothing of his campaign," he added significantly.

Joanna smiled over the rim of her coffee cup. "So true. Your plans for a frozen baby-food line is ingenious, Swain. We'd all love to hear about it."

"If you need a child model, Benj is available for a reasonable sitting fee," Peter immediately offered.

"I'm sure Swain has some baby in mind," Joanna interceded with a warning look. "Or perhaps some other idea."

"Yes, I do," Swain informed them proudly. "I plan to use *my* picture on the labels."

To Trey's horror, the Clancys began to laugh, uproariously, sidesplitting guffaws that nearly knocked them off their chairs. He hid his face in his hands in a silent moment of mourning. After all they'd been through together, they were going to wreck everything in this final hour, with the contract at his elbow!

"I don't understand the levity," Swain protested, his fork clanking to his plate.

"You weren't joking?" Granny Dot demanded in disbelief.

Swain stiffened in his seat. "No, I was not."

"Swain, darling, it wasn't our intention to insult you," Joanna said consolingly. "The notion just seems silly to us."

"It's my chance to be remembered, to be immortal!" he explained defensively. "I sell millions of dollars' worth of frozen foods annually, and do my consumers know me? No!"

Granny Dot peered at him through her spectacles. "But do they want to know you?"

"I just imagined they would!" he returned huffily.

"But don't they put babies on baby-food packages?" Peter reasoned.

"Your face is pretty wrinkled up," Benji said doubtfully, patting Swain's back in consolation. "Nobody will think you're a baby."

"Of course they won't! I'm nearly sixty."

"Well, young parents won't identify with your old face," Granny Dot warned.

Swain swiftly turned to Trey. "You think it's a brilliant idea, don't you, son?"

Trey couldn't tell this man another lie. "Though my in-laws can be a little crass in their delivery, their honesty is refreshing," he said with a twinge of apology. "I don't think it is the wisest course for your campaign, either. I've done everything but double back flips to get your account—"

"Has he ever!" Granny Dot blurted out dolefully.

"But I had every intention of steering you away from the idea once you signed on, or at the very least, of scaling down your picture to postage-stamp size." Swain opened his mouth to speak, but Trey stopped him with a halting palm. "I should've told you my feelings right from the start. But I respect you, wanted to work with you, so I skirted into the gray area of half-truths. Now, if you feel that Creative Works can't satisfy your company's needs, you can forget the contract and finish your pie in peace."

"Don't feel bad, Swain," Madeline hastened to add. "Surely you see your immortality in the faces of your children and your grandchildren."

Swain stroked his narrow face with a sigh of resignation. "This revelation comes as a bit of a surprise, Trey, but of course I want you to handle the account. I signed the papers, didn't I?"

Trey reared back in his chair. "You did? But when?"

"Right after our tour of the wine cellar. Spotted them on the buffet and knew I'd be departing early, so I just signed them. Where were you?"

"Down in the cellar with my lovely *bride,*" he replied lightly, his eyes sending the Clancys a silent message. A little truth was good for the soul, especially concerning Swain's ad campaign. But total frankness on personal matters was a different issue altogether. Swain had no right to expect him to be married in the first place. And besides, it looked like he and Madeline were soon going to make that illusion a reality, anyway.

Everyone pitched in to clean up the kitchen after dinner, then Trey and Swain settled into the family room to watch football on television. Trey distinctly remembered stretching out in the recliner, remembered the kickoff, remembered drinking another glass of dandelion deluxe. At what point he closed his eyes was a mystery, but close them he did. When he opened them, the game was over, the evening news was droning on the screen and the room was deserted.

Trey lunged out of the sinfully comfortable chair with a start. It was the exact site of Granny Dot's snoring fit last night. Oh, how they must have chuckled at his expense, no doubt dubbing him "sleepyhead" forevermore! He stepped up into the kitchen to find a note for him on the counter from Swain. The ladies had taken him to the airport. He would be in touch soon.

So where were Mad and the boys?

The basement door was ajar, so he headed down the stairs. Sure enough, there was a light on in Mad's office. Naturally, she would have a million details to catch up on. He quelled his territorial instincts, reminding himself that she seemed quite open to the idea of joining his work force, of funnelling her incredible talents into a partnership for two. He'd just peek inside for a quick hello and goodbye. With Swain gone, there was no reason for him to stay the night in the top bunk, test his willpower concerning Mad—so near, yet so far, down at the other end of the hallway.

He stood just outside the office, his lips primed with a greeting. But his voice froze in his throat as he took in the office hubbub from the basement shadows. Mad and the boys were in here all right, too busy to even notice him. But it wasn't Madeline who was sitting behind the computer, hammering at the keys, checking schedules, calling out dates and husband numbers. It was Peter, the twelve-year-old whiz kid!

12

TREY STOOD DUMBFOUNDED as he took in the Just Like a Wife operation in all it's glory. There was no mistaking who was the organizational whiz in the Clancy family, it was Peter. He was arranging everything, from the dry cleaning to the personal nights on the town. Theater tickets for Three. A new stove for Four. The furnace man for One. Peter had names, numbers, times—the works. Madeline, with Benji's backup, was filling in the charts, tacking notes to the bulletin boards. His first instincts about Mad had been right. She *couldn't* pull of the superwife-supersexed-superentrepreneur image she reflected. It was a huge sham!

"Hi, Five!" Benji squeaked suddenly. He scampered over and pulled Trey inside.

Trey stood in the center of the office, glaring at Mad. "You are a fake wife in every sense of the word, aren't you?"

"I was going to explain everything," she sputtered with flying hands.

"Better late than never," he invited evenly, folding his arms across his chest.

"Well, as you can see, this miracle worker doesn't work alone. Just Like a Wife is a family business. We all do our share. Mom is our craft lady, Granny Dot does the heavy cooking, Peter does the organizing—with Benji's help."

"What exactly do you do?"

"I stand on the front lines, with the public-relations job. I carry out the duties, keep up the morale. After all, what upscale bachelor would want to hire the whole Clancy family to look after them? People would laugh. It's up to me to reflect the cool image of the supermaid homemaker, give a husband something to brag about."

"Great plan," he congratulated her acerbically. "Guess nothing is really as it seems."

"Well, not the business details, anyway," she agreed on a contrite note. "Even when you caught sight of me in your bedroom last night, it was really closer to morning than night. I wasn't tucking the boys in, I was rousing them for work. This operation takes hours, and having you and Swain around made things more difficult than usual."

"So what you're telling me is that I've fallen in love with a whole family!" he thundered. "That Madeline the superwoman doesn't really exist." He moved over to the bulletin boards, stopping at the one labeled Five. He understood now how Dot knew his mother was a hairdresser. Vital statistics, intimate facts were all posted on index cards for easy perusal by any of them. Each board held the same sort of profile. "Somebody did some homework."

"Amazing the background check a guy can do with a computer and a telephone," Peter bragged, swiveling around in his chair.

"Nobody could take care of five men and live to tell the tale!" she lamented, trailing behind him. "After Dad died, we needed a major supplement to the family income. Pooling our resources seemed like the logical step. I started off with One and soon had a string of needy husbands, eager to pay for a platonic wife. As an advertising whiz you understand about product desirability. I seemed like the logical front person for our corporation." She laughed a little, hoping he'd join in. When he didn't, she continued in a somewhat huffy voice. "I wanted to tell you so many times, but you've made such an issue over my perfection. Made it clear that you love my image." Biting her lip, she shook her head forcefully. "I was so afraid I'd lose you when you found out the truth!"

"Ah, the ass I made of myself in front of your family!" he moaned, slapping his forehead. "You should've stopped me, Mad!"

"I tried to rein you in," Mad asserted.

"You should've tried harder. Cut off my big speech. No wonder your mother was ready to roast me!"

"I couldn't risk it," she reasoned. "You never would've been able to hide your irritation from Swain during dinner. He would've wondered what was wrong, and you would've blamed me for that, too!"

She was right on that score. And it only made him angrier. "Just when I thought I'd caught up with you, that we were in step together, I find out that you were miles ahead of me all the way!"

"We still are in step. Still in love," she cried out in protest.

"I don't even know the real you," he sputtered in fury. "To your city dates you're the sassy siren with the sultry voice and the dandelion nightcaps. To your husbands you're the cool, capable caregiver."

"The truth is somewhere in between," she confessed. "I wanted to tell you that I had backup, but you were so hung up on my perfection, so insecure about marrying a woman who fell short of your expectations. Darn it, I wanted you so badly, I was willing to try anything!"

"It blows me away that you could keep up this pretense, after all the things we discussed, all we've shared."

"I didn't want to lose you," Madeline insisted.

"I hate being tricked," he said roughly. "I told you so in many different ways. Even confided in you about Bonny. That humiliating trip." He hung his head, shoving his hands into his pockets.

"I didn't mean for things to progress this far, Trey."

"This is what I get for letting go," he lashed back. "For accepting the no-strings trust you offered."

"Well, you have to admit we did well by you," she returned with a snap in her eyes. "Swain left a happy man. You have your contract."

"You can expect a check in the mail for that," he promised tightly, moving for the door.

"Oh, so we're back to paying for everything," she said scornfully, following him out of the room.

Trey turned back at the foot of the stairs. "Yes, we are!"

"Well, I think you better have one long muse, Mr. Creative Works," she shouted at his back as he stormed up the stairs. "I may not be perfect, but I'm a darn good catch. I'm a good catch because when I go to bat for somebody, I always come through, see?"

TREY WANDERED INTO the Skyline Towers lobby later on that evening with his suitcase in hand, intending to retreat to his apartment for a nice long sulk.

"Oh, Mr. Turner!" Martin called out from behind him. "Happy Thanksgiving."

"Same to you, Martin," Trey returned quietly.

"Weren't expecting you until tomorrow," the doorman went on conversationally.

Trey smiled wanly. "I finished my business early."

"Business on Thanksgiving." Martin shook his head. "No wonder you're at the top of your field. Shall I take your case upstairs?"

"No, I can manage."

"I thought you'd be joining the others in the grill."

"It's closed today, isn't it?"

"To the public. But some of the tenants are having a turkey dinner in there. Victor Hess arranged it, I believe." Scanning Trey's indecisive face, he added, "I'm sure they'd enjoy the company."

Trey relinquished the case and rapped on the locked glass door leading to the grill. With a welcoming smile, Eddie ushered him inside. "Join the party!"

Trey scanned the small crowd clustered around a long buffet table of food, recognizing many of his fellow tenants.

"Well, look what the bartender dragged in," Gina exclaimed cheerily.

Vic took one look at him and released a groan. "Oh, no."

"Thanks a lot," Trey grumbled, already regretting that he'd stopped in.

Vic joined him at the bar, giving him a slap on the back. "You know what I mean, man. You were supposed to return tomorrow, the happiest man in Manhattan."

Trey leaned against the bar with a deep sigh of resignation.

Eddie stepped up to pour him a martini. "We would've invited you—"

"But you know that I usually bury myself in work during the holidays," Trey finished without rancor.

"It is your habit," Eddie agreed, openly relieved by Trey's attitude. "And Vic said you had plans of your own this year."

"Yeah. Entertaining Swain." Falling in and out of an engagement. Losing the woman of his dreams.

"What went wrong?" Vic asked, edging onto a stool beside Trey. "Swain catch on to the scam?"

"No, he's already winging home to California, none the wiser."

"Something's got you down," Vic prodded.

"Well, I proposed to Mad—"

"Terrific!"

"Then I found out that I'd have to marry the whole family to get the woman I wanted. Talk about a case of false advertising! It takes all the Clancys to run the Just Like a Wife show."

Vic grimaced. "Is that all?"

"That's everything! Mad isn't who she says she is. Hell, I don't know if she can even cook," he confided bleakly.

"I knew you'd end up in trouble with that objective theory on the perfect wife," Vic scolded.

"I was only trying to make the best deal for myself," Trey shot back.

"This isn't even about perfection," Vic went on. "Stop and think, Trey. You were attracted to Mad even before you found out that she was your supermaid, right?"

"Right," he begrudgingly admitted.

"You were so determined not to become involved with any woman, so verbal about it that you needed to justify falling for Madeline. Hence, you chose the perfect-wife excuse."

"Oh, c'mon!"

"It's true. Instead of just admitting that you'd fallen in love like the rest of us do, you explained it away by claiming that you'd discovered a flawless woman too great to pass up. You wanted us to know that even the rough, tough Trey Turner couldn't help but succumb to her impeccable charms."

"Sounds like a case of good old love to me," Gina chimed in, giving Trey a bolstering pat on the arm.

"Whipped-pup syndrome," Vic diagnosed once again.

"Jeez!" Trey crinkled his eyes to block out the jury of his peers. They were right on all counts. Hearing it in clear terms made it impossible to deny.

"This perfect-wife theory is for the birds," Eddie chimed in. "Especially considering just how far you are from being perfect-husband material."

Trey opened his eyes to find that Eddie had set the telephone down on the bar in front of him. "I'll call her." His three friends hovered close as he punched in Mad's Tuckahoe number. It was picked up on the fourth ring.

Trey's face flooded in relief as he connected with the familiar voice on the other end of the wire. "Hey, Benji. This is Trey."

"Oh, hi, Five. You still mad at us?"

"No, kid. And I was never mad at you personally."

"Good."

"And I haven't forgotten about the Barney toy," he attempted to mumble privately, to no avail.

"Good."

"Put your sister on the line."

"I can't."

"Why not?" he demanded anxiously.

"She's over at One's house."

"At this hour?" Trey gritted his teeth. Another husband in the way again.

"She's cleaning up or something. And getting my wagon back," he added with a whine. "It's mine and that man shouldn't have it overnight."

Trey fought to swallow his disappointment. "Well, tell her I called. Tell her to call me," he amended. "No matter what time she gets home."

"I dunno . . . She was really hollerin'. Said you're a big oaf. Said she wouldn't marry you if you were the last . . . Just a minute, Five. She called you something and I can't remember what. Peterrrr! What Maddy call Five again? What was that jungle ape thing?"

Trey clenched the receiver in a death grip, smiling tightly at the hopeful circle around him. Thankfully, this wasn't a speaker phone. No one knew what a beating he was taking.

"Yo, Five!" Peter's breathless voice came on the line.

"Hi, Peter."

"You calling for Madness?"

"I'm not so sure anymore."

"Ah, don't mind Benj. He got it all wrong."

Trey snorted. "Tell me another one."

"Yeah, I guess it's a little late in the game to be scamming you, isn't it?"

"Just want you to know we'll be getting together for those glasses this week."

"Technically, Swain signed of his own free will."

"Maybe, but you boys did a splendid job. A deal's a deal."

"You're all right, Five."

"So are you."

"About Madness—"

"I have her message loud and clear. Not much was lost in Benji's translation. Good night, Peter." Trey set the receiver back in its cradle.

"Well?" Eddie demanded anxiously.

Trey paused a moment to swallow the reality. "It's over. Kaput. *Fini.*"

Vic groaned again, burying his face in his hands.

Trey raised his martini into the air for a toast. "To Madeline Clancy and all of her husbands. May they all live happily ever after."

"I TOLD HIM HE SHOULD break down and visit you, Maddy," Vic said placatingly the following Friday night.

It had been a week and a day since her holiday flare-up with Trey, and they hadn't spoken a word to each other since. Madeline had just stopped by Vic's apartment to pick up her portrait. This visit to the city would be her last for a long time. There was no new Number Five yet, but Mad was sure it would be someone from Tuckahoe. As for her personal husband hunt, she'd pulled the plug on that fiasco indefinitely.

"He wouldn't even take my calls." She sighed, moping at her own profile on the canvas. Had she really ever been that happy, with eyes full of sparkle and hope? "I didn't mean the things I said about him. And I certainly didn't expect them to be passed along!"

A grin split Vic's round face. "He's been called lots of names in his day. I think he's brooding because nothing was exactly as he perceived it to be. And Trey, like the rest of us, really likes to be right."

"We overwhelmed him," she lamented. "I said it all along—the Clancys are just too much for a man to take in a sudden large dose. It's part of the reason why I wanted his apartment for dating. The plan was to make sure my man had fallen hard before exposing him to the brood. Trey got it full force. Not only was our relationship still in its early stages, but he had to face all the Clancys at once, overnight, rely on them to play his family."

"You want him back, don't you?"

Her cheeks grew pink. "Yes! But if he's not sure he wants me, I'm not going to rattle him into submission," she added on a petulant note.

"Well, I left him down in the grill about twenty minutes ago. He and Eddie have their heads together on that bachelor guide they're collaborating on. I think we should get him up here, find out how he feels."

"I think Trey's about finished with expressing his feelings," she predicted doubtfully. "How on earth are you going to force his hand?"

Vic picked up the telephone. "It won't be all that hard. Just a matter of pushing the right button." He pushed several buttons on the phone and sent her a wink. "Hi, Eddie, it's me. Could you give Trey a message, please? Tell him to bring up a bottle of champagne. No, the good stuff. I'm really celebrating. I'm

Madeline's new fifth husband! That's right. We're just sealing the deal up here. Okay. Thanks."

Madeline's laughter rang out as Vic hung up. "At the very least, it should bug him a little."

"A little?" Vic rasped. "I bet he shoots up here without the aid of an elevator!"

A few short minutes later there was a pounding on the door. Vic gave her a thumbs-up signal and swung it open. "Hey, Trey, where's the champagne?"

Trey barreled inside, his empty hands balled into fists. He looked a lot like his hippie pal in a frayed shirt and wrinkled cotton slacks.

"Hello, Trey," Madeline greeted him warmly. "I like the new rumpled-author look."

"I've been taking care of my own things this week," he informed her roughly. "An inconvenience, but far less complicated."

"Well, thanks for finding the time to take the boys shopping," she ventured. "Peter loves both pairs of glasses, and Benji won't go to sleep without his new stuffed Barney and transistor radio."

His dark encircled eyes sliced through her. "I stick to the bargains I make."

"So do I!" she flared, her civil manner evaporating. "I was a great wife to you, from beginning to end."

He sighed, shoving his hands in his pockets. "Well, if you're anxious for me to get my just desserts, you won't have long to wait."

Her forehead furrowed in confusion. "Oh?"

"Swain called me last night. To ask for your mother's hand in marriage."

Madeline gasped in pleasure. "How marvelous!"

"Didn't know who else to call. Figured I was the male head of the household. What a laugh, huh?"

"Oh, Trey," she clucked in frustration and regret.

"I told him she was a fine woman and it would be a wonderful match," he reported. "He plans to contact her tonight."

"Thank you for that," she murmured. "She's just crazy about him."

"Well, I think it's only right that I confess my bachelorhood soon. Make it clear that this was my scheme and that your mother had nothing to do with it. Wouldn't want another relationship spoiled by secrets."

"Nothing has to be spoiled," Madeline protested. "You're just too dense to see beyond your fantasies of the ideal marriage."

"Ideal?" he repeated in a growl. "You take on this caveman as your new Five and you talk to me about ideal fantasies?"

"You forget that I am looking for a platonic husband here. Vic's the perfect new Five. He knows all about the Clancy system and doesn't care who does what," she informed him smugly. "That makes him a most exceptional husband—my new favorite, hands down."

"Husbands, husbands—is that all you think about?" he railed, shaking a clenched fist.

"Yeah, so what's it to ya?" Madeline stood tall as he advanced, hovering over her in an aura of after-shave and fury.

Grasping her chin in his fingers, he stared down at her for a long, searing moment. "It's everything to me," he admitted huskily. "I can't go on without you. I can't go on as we were. I simply can't go on at all!"

"Were you ever going to come and tell me that?" she demanded.

He nodded ruefully. "I was. It's just taken me time to recover, to see the light. I'm one of those overbearing apes from the jungle, remember?"

"I didn't say you were overbearing," she objected.

"I appreciate it."

She moved back, eyeing him suspiciously, as he tried to reach for her. "How do I know you mean it, about coming for me?"

"Step across the hall and take a look at the apron I bought for you," he invited with a devilish grin.

"Hah! There's a tired old line!"

"I promise you I'm a new and improved man, Mad. A wiser lover who is making you the same offer all over again. Marry me. Forget about all these other guys."

His offer warmed her heart. She stared up into his needy eyes, seeking the proper response. "I need to work, to grow, Trey."

"I think Creative Works can provide enough challenge to keep you totally occupied," he swiftly shot back.

"But I am accustomed to keeping my own crazy hours."

"So am I."

"I'm bored easily. I wouldn't be good in a routine position."

"When you're tired of one coast, you can just jet off to light up the other."

"I am also accustomed to being the boss," she tossed in with a wry look.

"Now, there's a bit of conflict that's not going to be smoothed over so easily," he conceded dubiously.

"Well, don't look so darn glum about it!" she reprimanded him. "Don't you remember who you're talking to? A Clancy! A Tuckahoe debater who is always looking for a scrap to keep things lively."

"So you will marry me," he sought to verify.

"Of course I will! I just wanted to settle the tough stuff first."

"Wanted to keep me on a string, you mean."

"Yeah, well, a little squirming is good exercise," she said lightly.

"Looks like I'll be the one getting the champagne," Vic announced with a shrug, heading for the door.

"I can't wait to tell my family!" she exclaimed in delight, hardly noticing his departure. "They're all crazy about you."

"So how will we explain this to Swain?" Trey wondered.

"We won't have to," she purred mischievously. "Not if we beat them to the altar."

His features lit up. "Say, you've got a point. He never need be the wiser about when we did it."

"Just so we *do* do it," she teased with a provocative flutter of her lashes.

"I happen to be pretty fast on my feet," he informed her. "A jogger, you know."

"If we can't outrun them, sleepyhead, we'll find a way to outfox them!"

Trey opened his mouth to protest, but the words were interrupted by a deep-throated, burning kiss. A kiss to be continued across the hall, if he had his way.

"So, are you going to invite me inside this time, Mad?" he asked against her moist, swollen lips.

"For a nightcap?"

"For the *night*, my sassy diva. That's the way we do it in the city."

Her silvery eyes gleamed with anticipation. "You're in for it all night long, all right. The sassy diva treatment with a Tuckahoe twist!"

HARLEQUIN® Temptation

Lost Loves

RIGHT MAN...WRONG TIME

Remember that one man who turned your world upside down? Who made you experience all the ecstatic highs of passion and lows of loss and regret. What if you met him again?

You dared to lose your heart once and had it broken. Dare you love again?

JoAnn Ross, Glenda Sanders, Rita Clay Estrada, Gina Wilkins and Carin Rafferty. Find their stories in Lost Loves, Temptation's newest miniseries, running May to September 1994.

In June, experience *WHAT MIGHT HAVE BEEN* by Glenda Sanders. Barbara had never forgotten her high school sweetheart—nor forgiven him. Richard had gotten another girl pregnant and dutifully married her. Now a single dad, he's back in town, hoping to recapture and rekindle...what might have been.

What if...?

Available in June wherever Harlequin books are sold.

Take 4 bestselling love stories FREE

Plus get a FREE surprise gift!

HARLEQUIN®
Temptation®
IS TEN!

Join the festivities as Harlequin celebrates
Temptation's tenth anniversary in 1994!

Look for tempting treats from your favorite
Temptation authors all year long. The celebration
begins with Passion's Quest—four exciting sensual
stories featuring the most elemental passions....

The temptation continues with Lost Loves, a sizzling
miniseries about love lost...love found. And watch for
the 500th Temptation in July by bestselling author
Rita Clay Estrada, a seductive story in the vein
of the much-loved tale, THE IVORY KEY.

In May, look for details of an irresistible offer:
three classic Temptation novels by Rita Clay Estrada,
Glenda Sanders and Gina Wilkins in a collector's
hardcover edition—free with proof of purchase!

After ten tempting years, *nobody* can resist

Temptation®

HARLEQUIN® *Temptation®*
IS TEN!

Join the festivities as Harlequin celebrates Temptation's 10th anniversary in 1994!

Look for tempting treats from your favorite Temptation authors all year long…. *Passion's Quest,* four exciting stories featuring the most elemental passions…followed by *Lost Loves,* a sizzling miniseries about finding your lost love. And in July, Rita Clay Estrada brings us Temptation's 500th book, *Forms of Love,* a seductive story in the vein of the much-loved tale *The Ivory Key.*

The celebrations continue with an irresistible offer! Three of your favorite Temptation novels are available in a beautiful collector's hardcover edition—free with 6 proofs of purchase!

> Rita Clay Estrada—The Ivory Key
> Glenda Sanders—Daddy, Darling
> Gina Wilkins—A Stroke of Genius